Lydia Barnes and the Mystery of the Broken Cross

Heather Gemmen Wilson

wesleyan
publishing
house

Indianapolis, Indiana

Copyright © 2007 by Wesleyan Publishing House
Published by Wesleyan Publishing House
Indianapolis, Indiana 46250
Printed in the United States of America

ISBN: 978-0-89827-351-9

Contents

For Mariya

A Note to You

When I was a girl living in the wide-open spaces of Oklahoma, I loved mystery stories. Sometimes, as I followed the adventures of my hero, Nancy Drew, the story was so intense that I could barely turn the pages to see what would happen next. Little did I know that I would someday experience many similar adventures of my own.

When I became a follower of Jesus, he opened the world to me. I began to see that it was not just storybook heroes who could have adventures—regular kids like I was could go out and do amazing things to make the world a better place. Remember, when you and I pray the Lord's Prayer saying "Thy will be done on earth as it is in heaven," God wants *us* to make that happen!

Now I'm pleased to introduce you to a wonderful new hero named Lydia Barnes. I know you'll be thrilled to follow her adventures in faraway places like Africa, Jamaica, and Jerusalem. As you do, remember this amazing truth—*Kids can change the world!*

I hope this book will be the beginning of your own adventure. I am looking forward to hearing about the awesome, creative things *you* will do to make a difference in your community and in the world.

Jo Anne Lyon
Executive Director
World Hope International

1

Blown Up

Lydia Barnes screamed, and the lights flickered back on.

"What happened?" someone yelled.

Lydia had no idea. She'd heard a deafening bang and lunged forward, sure she was about to be blown up. She had bumped into something but didn't know what.

Lydia looked at her hands. Brown ooze dripped from her fingers.

She looked at the floor and saw a broken lamp and a fallen body.

She looked up at the small crowd of people in the lobby of the Christian Hope Guesthouse in Jerusalem, where she and her dad had been mingling with the other guests—and all eyes were on her. "I . . . I . . ." she mumbled, "I think it was me. I think it's my fault."

✝   ✝   ✝

"It's my fault" were words fourteen-year-old Lydia Barnes generally tried to avoid. The gutsy American teenager didn't like being in the hot seat, and she usually did everything she could to avoid getting there.

But this was different. Something terrible had happened.

"Marcus," she said, bending down over her friend, not sure what to do with her sticky hands.

Marcus was one of the teens traveling with a group called Youth Around the World. They had arrived at the guesthouse just a few hours before Lydia on a tour of the Holy Land. Marcus was nearly six feet tall, almost as tall as Lydia's dad, and had the broad shoulders of a defensive lineman on a football team. With his mass of black curly hair and his perfectly black eyes, Marcus could appear a bit wild at times. But his sweet smile and smooth, milk chocolate skin made him look positively innocent. And he had been making Lydia laugh all evening.

Until now.

"Marcus," she said again.

He groaned, rolled over, and looked at her gooey hands hovering inches above his face. "You didn't squash the last brownie, did you?" he asked.

Lydia stared at him for a moment, then looked at her hands. With everyone watching, she placed one finger in her mouth and tasted the chocolate goo. "That," she said firmly, "was the best brownie I've ever had!"

Marcus sat up, grinning. "Remind me never to pop a balloon near you again."

✝ ✝ ✝

No one could blame Lydia for freaking out. She and her dad had made it through the madness of security screening at the Tel Aviv airport where people seemed to think that every piece of gum and bottle of water held a secret bomb, so what did they expect? She'd heard a bang and naturally assumed it was a bomb.

Mrs. Oliver, the guesthouse host, shooed them all away with a severe stare and then cleaned up the broken glass. Lydia's dad, Frank Barnes, went right back to talking with two British archae-ologists who were taking a break from their work in the Negev for a little holiday in Jerusalem—it was just one more week until Christmas. Lydia glanced over at her dad while stopping another blow from Marcus's pillow. She was glad to see her dad was wearing the black, zippered hoody with wild white designs all over the front. She had bought that for him as an early Christmas present while they were in Amsterdam a few days earlier, and he'd picked out some faded, loose jeans. What a difference from the plaid button-down shirts and khaki pants most of the other dads were wearing. One dad from Australia was even wearing ugly green cords!

"So which one is yours?" Lydia asked Marcus, yanking the pillow out of his hand so he'd quit hitting her.

The people in Marcus's group were from all over the United States—fifteen teenagers and four adults.

"Are you kidding?" Marcus said. "He's not here. Maybe if he was cool like your dad, I would've let him come." And he hit her with another pillow.

Lydia giggled and hit him back.

"Ahem."

Lydia looked up to see Katherine Oliver staring down at her. Maybe if a twelve-legged, slimy alien from some bizarre inter-galactic planet had come to earth to study humans, it could look as disgusted as Mrs. Oliver did at this moment. But she wasn't an alien. She was a middle-aged Christian woman with too much makeup and lots of gaudy jewelry.

"I'm sorry, ma'am," Lydia said, but she didn't really know what she was supposed to be apologizing for. Was it for the lamp? Or the noise? Or for simply existing?

"Show a little more discretion, if you please," the woman said. Whatever that meant.

Lydia might have felt miserable if she weren't so happy. Marcus hit her with a pillow again, and she saw Martin Oliver give her a wink. Clearly, Mrs. Oliver was the only grump in the room. Mr. Oliver was a tall and frail man with the thinnest, palest lips Lydia had ever seen. He hadn't spoken once since Lydia met him, but he smiled a lot.

"Yoo-hoo!" Mrs. Oliver now called to another teenager at the other end of the room, her voice carrying above all the others. "Don't touch that vase, please." Then off she went to place a pillow firmly between two other teenagers who were talking on the couch. "No need to sit so close together," she said. "And button up that shirt, missy."

"She's got *serious* problems," the girl said a bit too loudly as soon as Mrs. Oliver swooped away.

Mr. Oliver winked again.

"Hey, everyone!" said a slim woman of about Lydia's dad's age. She was the guide of Marcus's tour group, and she wore black cotton pants with leather in the front, a soft black shirt, a black leather vest, and high-heeled boots. Her classy glasses were hand decorated with gold and silver squiggles, and her shoulder-length hair was layered and spiky. She might have been a fashion designer in Amsterdam, but she was actually a historian and Bible teacher from Monterey, California. "Good news!" she said.

"Of great joy?" asked Lydia's dad, and Lydia thought of the famous Bible passage about the angels announcing the birth of Jesus to the shepherds.

"Why, thank you, Frank," Dr. Erwin said slyly. "Do I look like an angel to you?"

So this was the famous Dr. Erwin. Lydia's dad had mentioned her a few times, always with a bit of a grin. Her full name was Skyblue Dawn Erwin, but Frank had told Lydia never to call her that. "Stick with 'Dr. Erwin,'" he'd advised.

"With all that leather," Frank said now, grinning, "more like a biker."

"I wouldn't know about that," said Dr. Erwin without cracking a smile, "though I trust you to be informed about anything that is noisy and grimy." Then she winked at Lydia.

Great. Someone with the same sense of humor as her dad. Now he'd never quit. Still, Lydia smiled.

"As I was saying," Dr. Erwin said, glaring at Frank with just the faintest of smiles. Frank pretended to zip his lips. "You'll never guess what Brenda found today."

Everyone turned to look at the Canadian college girl, who happened to be right beside Lydia. Brenda was fun and independent and afraid of nothing. She was volunteering at the guesthouse for a few months to earn her room and board, and Lydia adored her sense of adventure. "Oh! Oh! Oh!" Brenda said. "Let me tell them!"

"Of course," Dr. Erwin said, bowing slightly.

"A historic Holy Land token!" Brenda whispered loudly into the now-quiet room. "You know, the mysterious Palestinian coin of 1927!"

"This coin is probably one of the most interesting topics debated among coin collectors," Dr. Erwin said. "It is sometimes referred to as the 'Souvenir Mil.' No one really knows why this particular item was made or whether it is a coin or some sort of token."

"Do you want to see it?" Brenda asked her audience.

"Of course we do!" Dr. Erwin said. "We won't believe you have it otherwise."

Brenda laughed. "It's out in my car," she said. "Come on, Lydia. I want some company."

Brenda pushed open the heavy wooden door, and the two girls stepped out into the darkness. A package wrapped in brown paper lay at the doorstop, and Lydia bent and picked it up without thinking.

"Hold up!" It was Lydia's dad. He was following them out the door and handing Lydia the white fuzzy coat he had bought her in Amsterdam. "I'm not letting you out alone this time of night. I'm coming with."

"Dad!" Lydia groaned, embarrassed. It wasn't even ten o'clock yet. She was glad for the coat, though; it couldn't have been more than forty-five degrees out there. She moved down the concrete steps out of the way of the others who were coming out the door, set the package on the bottom step, and pulled the jacket on.

A bright lamp shone above them, and the street that had been so busy earlier in the day was nearly empty. Only a few cars were parked along the road, including a white Ford Focus at the end of the block. Iron gates covered the doors to the many neighboring shops that were packed tightly together—tall stone buildings that looked ancient and forbidding. Hardly any other people were out walking.

"I may as well come too," Dr. Erwin said, moving in step beside Frank. "I want to hear about your scuba diving experience. Did you say you went diving in South America?"

"South *Africa*," Frank replied, his breath turning white as he spoke. "I dove deep into the home of the most savage beasts of the sea . . ." he said, holding up his hands in a dramatic pose, "solo!"

Lydia groaned at her dad's lame humor, but Dr. Erwin grinned and urged him on. "And did you meet up with any of these savage beasts?"

The door of the guesthouse was still open, and some others from the group filed out, obviously interested in Frank's story. Marcus ran out in his T-shirt, followed by the same girl who had made fun of Mrs. Oliver, along with the boy she had been whispering with on the couch. A few of the other Americans and both the Australian kids followed close behind.

Frank waited until everyone was crowded around. "I've been scuba diving for years," he continued, then gestured for Brenda to lead on. The small gang walked down the sidewalk, slipping and sliding on the thin layer of frost, toward the Focus. "But I had never encountered any big creatures until this dive."

Lydia had heard at least three million times how Frank had been swimming next to a pack of blacktip sharks and lived to tell about it, so she pulled her iPod from her pocket and stuck in her ear buds. She clicked on her favorite Hawk Nelson song and cranked up the volume. Lydia fell nearly to the back of the crowd, trailed only by a couple of American guys, who were barely shuffling forward at all.

After a moment, Frank, who had been walking backward to face his small audience, took on a look of perfect terror, and Lydia understood why everyone loved his storytelling so much. She belted out a laugh that must have been heard by those same sharks at the bottom of the sea.

Suddenly everyone whipped around, each of their faces holding as much terror as Frank's. Lydia pulled the buds from her ears.

Something was wrong.

The first thing Lydia saw was that the American teenagers behind her had fallen down. When she looked past them, she noticed that the front door of the guesthouse—the door to the guesthouse they'd just walked out of—was blown away. The people inside were staring back at them through the open space. The steps they had just walked down were now a pile of rubble.

Suddenly everyone was moving at once. Mrs. Oliver ran out of the house and Frank ran toward it. Lydia began running and was the first to reach the fallen boys. She tore off her jacket and placed it under his head and shoulders, fuzzy side up, and then carefully wrapped her sweatshirt around his bleeding arm, which was bent in an awkward direction. She didn't even feel the chilly air on her arms as she rubbed the sweat from the boy's forehead with her sleeve. *Andrew*, she thought his name was.

When she finally looked up again, her father was a few feet away leaning over another teenage boy, and Mrs. Oliver was walking around squeezing her hands together. All the others were either huddled down the street by Brenda's car or were still inside the guesthouse, cowering on far side of the front room. Mr. Oliver was nowhere to be seen.

If only the ambulances would arrive.

Mrs. Oliver brought water to the boy Lydia was caring for, but did not look at Lydia. *I'm sorry*, Lydia wanted to say. This time she knew what she was apologizing for. *I'm sorry I laughed.* She hadn't known the boom she'd dimly heard over the music blaring in her ears was a bomb. She hadn't known her dad's shocked expression was not part of the crazy story he was telling.

"Is Mr. Oliver okay?" Lydia asked Mrs. Oliver meekly.

"Yes, he is in the house," the woman replied before walking toward the guesthouse.

Suddenly Lydia started to tremble. Someone had bombed the building they'd just been in! If they hadn't gone outside to see the coin . . . She wanted to call out to her dad but knew he had more important things to do. She looked down at the boy she'd been tending. Blood from his arm was soaking through the sweatshirt, and now his eyes were fluttering shut. Crying wouldn't help, but Lydia couldn't stop the tears. "Hold on," Lydia whispered to him. "The ambulance will be here in a minute. Just keep your eyes open!"

A blanket fell over Lydia's shoulders, and a paramedic gently moved her aside. When had an ambulance arrived? "I've got him," he said in accented English. "Get yourself in the house where it's warm."

Lydia nodded, weeping uncontrollably now, and walked toward the side door to the guesthouse, where others were filing in and out. She found an unoccupied corner of the kitchen and curled up, trying to think of nothing.

When you try to think of nothing, of course, thoughts flood through your brain faster than whitewater down the Colorado River. Lydia recalled the last thirty-six hours of her life that had brought her from the wet heat of Africa to the dry chill of the Middle East.

One moment she had been in the Liberian airport hugging Ben—the missionary kid who had become her best friend in a matter of weeks. Together they'd undertaken a sometimes perilous, sometimes heartbreaking, ultimately victorious treasure hunt. In the next moment she had been hugging her dad in a Dutch hotel lobby, thanking him for giving her the best present she could ever imagine—the heart-shaped diamond necklace she now wore around her neck—and then exploring the canal-lined streets of that historic city. Now she was hugging her own knees in the rubble of a Christian guesthouse somewhere in the middle of a war zone during the holiday season that was supposed to bring peace on earth.

When Lydia's dad had first presented the idea of traveling the world together so he could serve as Director of Critical Issues for

Global Relief and Outreach—usually just called GRO—Lydia hadn't considered long. Hmmm . . . study half a day with a tutor while exploring foreign countries—or sit through boring middle school classes all day long in Indiana? Easy choice. So before she could even finish that trimester, she, her dad, and the newly hired tutor had swooped off to Africa for trip number one.

But right about now Indiana sounded like paradise.

2
Displaced

The next thing Lydia knew her dad was shaking her awake. "Come on, Peachoo," he said. "I've found us another place to spend the night."

Lydia stood up, rubbing sleep from her eyes, and followed Frank out of the guesthouse to a cab that was parked alongside the road, just past Brenda's car. It was still dark, and frost covered the sidewalk and street, except where the bomb had gone off. Lydia could see the frosty footprints their group had made earlier. She also noticed litter waving lightly in the breeze along the edge of the curb and graffiti on the walls of the buildings around her. It must have been there before, but she hadn't noticed.

"I've got all our stuff in the trunk already," Frank said, pulling his daughter close.

Lydia hadn't even thought of their luggage. All she could think of was whether another bomb would go off and blow them to Timbuktu. She hurried into the cab. The clock said 12:17. It felt much later.

"All the hotels I called were full," Frank said to Lydia after he'd instructed the driver where to take them, "so we have to stay in a stable."

From the corner of her eye she saw him looking at her, but she didn't look back. It wasn't funny.

As if reading her mind, her dad said, "Sorry, Peachoo." He was quiet as the cab drove slowly down the street. He concentrated on carefully reading road signs, many of which were in three different languages—Hebrew, English, and Arabic. "It should be right around here."

"What are we looking for?" Lydia asked. They were moving into an area with more traffic and driving alongside a huge wall. Many people were walking beside the wall, and taxis were honking, even though it was the middle of the night.

"We're looking for the Dung Gate. If we get dropped off there, we should be able to find the guesthouse we're staying at just inside the walls."

"The *what* gate? Dad, where are you taking us?"

"It's called Shalom Guesthouse. There was a Jewish man in the crowd after the bombing, and he and I got talking. He offered to open up a room for us at his small guesthouse. We'll be there in a minute. It's just inside the wall, in the Jewish Quarter."

"Oh, good!" Lydia said, feeling a little better now that they had people looking out for them. "I like Jewish people!"

"Really?" Frank asked as other cabs whizzed around them, beeping. Their driver was slowing down and turning at a sharp corner. "I didn't know you knew any."

"Well, I read some books by a guy named Chaim Potok," Lydia said. It felt weird to be talking like this. Here they were, having a normal conversation and riding in normal traffic, when they had nearly died a couple of hours ago and the Olivers were still dealing with the trauma of the damage to their guesthouse. She wanted to slow time down, but it kept tugging her forward.

"*Cha*im," Frank corrected, making a sound like he was clearing his throat.

"Whatever. And I also watched *Fiddler on the Roof.*"

"Those were Russian Jews in the early twentieth century," Frank said. "But, to use your very wise word: whatever. I'm glad you like Jewish people."

The cab stopped just outside the gate, and Frank and Lydia got out. The wall towered above the gate itself, more than twice as high, and Lydia could see the outline of turrets in the dark sky. The gate appeared as a small hole in the gray stone wall, wide enough for about two small cars to pass side by side and high enough for maybe a school bus to squeeze under. Even at this time of night, many cars were crawling in and out in the slow, heavy traffic.

The sidewalk ended at the gate, and they walked through on an asphalt road, weaving between the cars, towing their suitcases behind them. On the other side, a tall man in a loose-fitting business suit and a skullcap—which looked like a piece of fabric just the right size to cover a bald spot—walked over to them, unsmiling. His dark hair was peppered gray.

Frank greeted him with a big crooked grin and held out a hand, but the man just scowled and rushed them down a narrow walkway surrounded by gray stone buildings.

"Thank you so much for making room for us at the last moment—" Frank said.

"Yes, yes," the man interrupted, waving a hand as if to make the talking go away. He led them up a few narrow steps into a grayish stone building that looked the same as the others except that a yellow porch light illuminated a sign over the door: Shalom Guesthouse. "Your room is there." He handed Frank a key and pointed to a door on the main floor. "Rest well."

"Um . . . right," Frank said. "Good night."

"A little different than the Olivers' guesthouse," Lydia remarked once they were in their room, a tiny space with two single beds. Not that she cared. She just wanted sleep.

"Yeah . . . " Frank said. He seemed to be thinking about something, but Lydia didn't try to find out what.

"Good night," she said with as much finality in her voice as their new host had given.

It turned out to be a good thing they were staying at Shalom Guesthouse, as far as Lydia was concerned. The first thing she saw when she went down for breakfast the next morning was the community computer, complete with Internet access. She couldn't live without her blog and instant messages and e-mail. Even so, it looked strange to have something so modern as a computer in this otherwise simple place.

The lobby was about the size of Lydia's living room back home. Its walls were covered in purple, silky cloth. Where the fabric overlapped, Lydia could see flakes of white coming off the stone beneath. The tile floor was old and cracked, though shiny clean. A stick of incense poked up from the lobby counter beside a small hand bell, and the sweet odor drifted past Lydia's nose.

Lydia sat at the computer desk, a narrow table stuck against the outside wall, and logged on. Her dad walked off to order breakfast in the small café, which was separated from the lobby by an arched doorway. There were about four small, round tables, each covered with purple cloth and surrounded by three chairs—and a larger table pressed against the wall with beverages, fruit, and bread.

Lydia saw that Ben wasn't online, so she couldn't IM him—it was 6:00 a.m. in Liberia. She wrote a quick e-mail instead:

ben . . . it's crazy here . . . i thought liberia was a war zone but it's totally different here . . . i almost got blown up by a bomb . . . i'm serious! . . . don't worry tho, i won't have as much fun here as i did there J lol luv, lyd

What she really wanted to write was that she had been scared out of her mind, but then Ben might think she was a wimp.

Besides, with the bright morning light streaming in through the windows on either side of the computer desk, she wasn't nearly as scared as she had been last night.

Lydia went on to important things: Kutless. As she was downloading music onto her iPod, her best friend, Amy, signed on . . . way back in Indiana.

thelid1: ames! is that really u???
Redhead2831: lid!!
thelid1: what r u doing up? isnt it like 1 am there?
Redhead2831: i'm chatting w/ tom
Redhead2831: tee hee
thelid1: tom? i thot u couldnt stand him
Redhead2831: hes changed a lot . . . hes matured
Ben signed on next.
grtbenmn: hi lid . . . i'm glad ur on
thelid1: ben!
thelid1: i just sent u a mssg
grtbenmn: k, ill check, but 1st i have to tell u something
thelid1: k
Redhead2831: g2g lid
Redhead2831: moms up
Redhead2831: ilu
thelid1: k bye
thelid1: ilu2
grtbenmn: shoot . . . g2g . . . ill send u a mssg

They both signed out at the same time.

"Who are you talking to?" a girl's voice said from behind Lydia.

Lydia turned around and saw a beautiful girl about her own age, with longer, darker hair than her own, covered with a cute, brown-and-white knit beanie. She wore faded jeans and a fluffy brown feather coat zipped right up to her chin. She wore just a little bit of makeup—mascara and blush—and it looked nice. But what caught Lydia's attention was the little smile that said, "I know you're up to no good—and I want to join you." The girl's small, oval eyes flitted back and forth over Lydia's face, as if she waited for some juicy gossip.

"Ummm . . . " Lydia said. "Just some friends."

The girl's eyes got big, and she quickly moved to the chair next to Lydia. "Some . . . ehr . . . *boy*friends?" the girl asked. The *ehr* sound the girl made was the only indication that English was not her first language. She didn't say "um" or "uh" as Lydia might have said while searching for the right word; and no English-speaking girl would forget the word *boyfriend*. But she didn't really have an accent, except maybe that she said her words carefully.

Lydia laughed. "No way!"

"How come you're . . . ehr . . . blushing?" The girl was still smiling, and she put her hand on Lydia's arm, as if they shared a private joke.

"I'm not blushing!" Lydia said. She forced herself to smile even though she hated it when people said she was blushing. It only made her blush more. She didn't want to start off on the wrong foot with this girl.

The girl shrugged. "Have it your way." She stuck out her hand. "I'm Sarah."

Lydia shook it. "I'm Lydia."

"So tell me everything!" Sarah said, leaning back in her chair. "Was it scary?"

"What? Writing to my friends?"

"No, silly! The . . . ehr . . ." She shot her fingers outward and made a sound like an explosion.

"Oh, that."

Apparently Sarah had heard about the bombing. That was the last thing Lydia wanted to talk about. She had just managed to convince herself she wasn't afraid, and she wasn't about to change that. And she for sure wasn't going to show this girl her fears.

"Listen," Lydia said, standing up. "I'd better go. My dad is waiting for me."

"I'll see you later, then," Sarah said, moving her chair aside. "I live here, so you can't get rid of me." She was probably trying to be funny.

"At least someone here is glad to have us," Frank said quietly. He and Lydia were sitting at a table eating breakfast. "Who's your new friend?"

"Sarah," Lydia said, and a cucumber almost slipped out of her mouth. She quickly chewed and swallowed it, and then asked, "Why aren't they glad to have us?"

"You have to understand the religious and political climate here," Frank began—and Lydia wished she hadn't asked the question. He'd probably lecture for a few years. "It's a tough place to live. People don't really know who to trust."

"They can trust us," Lydia said. She reached for another pita bread and began stuffing it with cucumbers and cream cheese spread. This stuff was good. "We're Christians."

"Actually, Jewish people don't much like Christian missionaries—for the same reason the Jews in Paul's time didn't like them."

She knew her dad wanted her to ask the question. "Why's that?"

Frank finished chewing before he answered. "Because if Christians are right that Jesus is the Messiah—"

"Which He is," Lydia said.

Frank nodded, "—then the whole Jewish way of life is upset. And some Christian missionaries can get, shall we say, overzealous about their work. It's not very attractive."

"If they don't like us, why did they let us stay here?"

Frank chuckled and took another bite. He chewed and swallowed before he answered. "They're good people, Lydia. Mr. Klein saw that we were in need and he offered assistance. He's not even making us pay for our stay. Good people do good things even if they don't feel like it."

Lydia looked over at Sarah, who was now on the computer. The two of them had at least one thing in common: do-gooder dads.

"Okay, Peachoo," Frank said. "Let's finish up here and get out to see some sights. But first we'll head over to the Olivers' to see how they're doing, digging out from the damage."

3
Creeped Out

ike so many of the buildings in Israel, the Christian Hope Center was made of white, unpainted stone. The tiny front yard was cement—the only grass Lydia had seen in Jerusalem was at a park—but the place had a certain charm with its white-pebbled walkway and iron gate. The center was run by the Olivers, whose guesthouse was just a few blocks away. Lydia could still taste the almond tea she had for breakfast as she stepped out of the cab, and that made everything seem a little more quaint.

"Lydia!" someone called to her.

"Brenda!" Lydia screamed with delight and ran to the college girl's arms. They had met only yesterday, but Lydia felt as if they were special friends. Maybe that's what happens when you almost die together. "Are you okay? Did you get hurt at all?"

"No, I'm fine. Everybody's fine," Brenda answered. "Some people are pretty banged up, but no one was killed."

"Everybody?" Lydia asked, her right arm wrapped around Brenda's waist.

"That boy you were helping has a badly broken arm, and he had to have a blood transfusion because he lost so much blood, but he'll be okay." Brenda kept her left arm around Lydia's shoulders as they walked toward to door to the center.

Lydia thought of the guesthouse that had been the target of the terrorist bomb yesterday. They had driven by it just a moment ago on their way to the Christian Hope Center and seen men in orange vests and white hardhats working to clear the rubble. It was strange to see that destruction over there, yet here everything seemed fine.

Frank walked behind Lydia and Brenda. "Did you manage to find a place to stay last night?" he asked.

"Yeah," Brenda said, "I stayed right here at the Christian Hope Center. Mr. and Mrs. Oliver did too."

"What about the others?" Lydia asked.

"I think the American tourists went to Novotel, but I don't know about the others." She winked at Lydia and squeezed her shoulder, knowing full well that Lydia's main concern was Marcus. Lydia grinned back. Good thing her dad was clueless. He liked to think of Lydia as a nine-year-old rather than a mature young lady.

"Oh, Frank!" Mrs. Oliver's pinched face appeared at the doorway. She stood beckoning him into the building. "I'm so glad you're here! We're all so rattled!"

"Yes, I can imagine," Frank said. He accepted her hug as soon as they were inside. Brenda and Lydia followed Frank inside. Brenda walked over to Mr. Oliver, who was in the back corner of the room doing something that looked like counting books, and Lydia went to her dad.

The room functioned as a large bookstore, selling pamphlets and other Christian literature, including a pile of books written by Martin and Katherine Oliver, titled *The Only True Path*. There was a huge, poster-sized photograph of the Olivers hanging above the cash register, and there were smaller pictures of the couple all around the store. Lydia wished Ben were here so she would have someone to gag with. She could just hear him: *They're a little into themselves, aren't they?*

"I'm so glad you're here!" Mrs. Oliver said again to Lydia's dad. "The police were hoping to talk to you. But they've left now."

"Did they find out who did it?" Frank asked.

"No. Not yet." Mrs. Oliver looked quickly at Lydia. "Darling, did you have a package in your hand when you went outside with Brenda?"

Brenda glanced up quickly.

"No," Lydia said. "I found it on the steps. I picked it up to give it to you, but then I set it down at the bottom of the steps when Dad gave me my coat." She felt her face go red. "I guess I forgot about it. I'm sorry. Was it important?"

Everyone stared at Lydia.

"You found a package?" Frank asked.

"The police believe that package held the bomb," Mrs. Oliver said. Her look was so intense that Lydia felt like Mrs. Oliver was blaming her, and her face got even hotter.

"Wow," Frank said. "If that package had been left by the door or, worse, brought inside, the damage would have been incredible. It scares me to death to think that bomb was in your hands, Lydia; but you saved the day!" He pulled her close in a hug and then leaned toward Mrs. Oliver, who was still eyeing Lydia. "If it's any comfort, the whole world is praying for you. Last night's bombing was the biggest item on the evening news back in the States."

"Yes, we've been talking to reporters all morning." Mrs. Oliver put her hand on Frank's arm, as if they were best friends, and said, "Americans attacked on Israeli soil! It's horrible!"

But to Lydia, Mrs. Oliver looked anything but horrified. At first Lydia couldn't figure out why the woman seemed so delighted by such an awful thing, but then she saw her glance at the pile of books she and her husband had written. Maybe Mrs. Oliver was seeing dollar signs, imagining how many books would sell because of all the attention they were getting.

But that wasn't fair. Mrs. Oliver couldn't possibly have been happy about the attack.

Mrs. Oliver followed Lydia's dad deeper into the store, which looked just like any Christian bookstore Lydia had been in back home. Lydia was tempted to browse—she loved reading—but she didn't dare leave her dad's side. She would have preferred to get out of the building altogether. What if someone *was* out to get the Olivers? There could be another bomb heading their way right now. Lydia tugged on his arm, hoping he'd head toward the door. But Frank shook her off and gave her a leave-me-alone look.

"What can we do to help?" Frank asked.

"Pray," Mrs. Oliver responded without even stopping to think. She was strolling after Frank with Lydia trailing behind, and Mr. Oliver and Brenda looked up from counting books as the three drifted toward them. Lydia couldn't bring herself to pick up any of the books even though some of her favorites were there— like The Chronicles of Narnia and *Anne Frank: The Diary of a Young Girl.* "The Enemy is attacking us," Mrs. Oliver continued, louder, "so we must be on the right track. We need to have our sword and shield ready!"

When they reached the music section, Lydia momentarily forgot they were on the verge of being blown up. Thousand Foot Krutch! DecembeRadio! NewsBoys!

"We sure are praying, Katherine," Frank replied, not a bit distracted by the Hawk Nelson display that Lydia couldn't take her eyes off. Frank put his hands on the edge of the display rack and leaned forward. Lydia was sure he didn't have a clue that he was leaning against an awesome picture of Jason Dunn, the band's lead singer. Mrs. Oliver was in the aisle on the other side of the display, and Mr. Oliver and Brenda were in the aisle behind her.

"That's why you've come to Jerusalem, isn't it?" Mrs. Oliver said with just a hint of a question in her voice. She leaned over and patted Frank's hand. "To find out how to pray for those of us dedicated to the Holy City."

"I will certainly pray for you," Frank said, resuming his walk. With his elbow off of poor Jason Dunn's face, Lydia was free to again stare at the love of her life. "But my main purpose is to figure out whether it would be useful for GRO to set up a ministry here to support the work of fine Christians like you. I'll begin by praying."

"That's always a good place to start," Brenda said.

"How refreshing!" Mrs. Oliver said, turning around to smile at her husband and nodding as if trying to get him to smile too. "Too many folks come over here trying to reinvent the wheel. We Christians shouldn't be in competition with each other." She smiled at Frank again. "The Christian Hope Center is already doing the most important work there is to be done, and the other missions that come in with their own agendas just undercut our work."

Lydia looked up from the CDs. "What is the most important work?" She immediately regretted asking the question, because Mrs. Oliver glared at her.

"Sharing the gospel, of course!" the woman nearly shouted. "The Jewish people just have to get it through their . . ." the pause was noticeable, and Lydia wondered what word she left out, ". . . heads that their Messiah has already come and—" She stopped herself. "Ah, but I'm preaching to the choir." She smiled at Frank knowingly.

"He's not in the choir," Lydia said, trying to lighten things up. "Have you ever heard him sing?"

Frank and Brenda laughed, but Mrs. Oliver only smiled—as sweetly as a snake. She beckoned to her husband. "Come, Martin. Let's show Frank the rest of the center."

Everyone headed toward a door behind the checkout counter, but a big stack of the Olivers' books caught Lydia's eye. There were about a dozen of them piled on the glass countertop beside a huge glossy picture of the Olivers. Beneath the counter was a display of religious jewelry. Lydia stopped and picked up one of the books. It seemed to be all about the idea that Jesus is the only way to heaven. It was all true, of course, but somehow the book seemed annoying anyway.

Lydia was halfway through reading the preface when she noticed how quiet it was in the bookstore. Creeped out, she quickly dropped the book and ran after the others.

Lydia bolted through the door toward her dad. Embarrassed, she tried to pretend she hadn't been rushing, but Brenda saw her and smiled.

They were in a gathering room with about a fifty chairs surrounding a small stage. It looked like the chamber choir room in her old middle school, except that this place had cushy chairs and stained glass windows. "We have worship services here on Sunday mornings and Sunday evenings," Mrs. Oliver said. "Martin preaches and I play the piano. We haven't yet found anyone who is able to run the sound system very well; please pray for that. Oh!" she said suddenly. "Maybe if you set up a ministry here *you* could help us."

Frank didn't answer. Instead he admired the building, then asked more questions about the ministry. Mrs. Oliver yapped on happily and Mr. Oliver waited patiently, but after five minutes or so, Brenda headed back to the bookstore. Lydia tugged on her dad's arm again, this time not so much afraid as bored.

"You can go on back to the bookstore with Brenda if you want," he said.

"Come on, Lydia," Mr. Oliver said, in a voice that sounded very much like Eeyore, "I'm going back there myself."

Lydia sighed and followed him back into the store. She wanted to get out of this place, but at least in the bookstore she had posters of her favorite bands to distract her.

But a moment later, boys were the last thing Lydia was thinking of.

1

Spun

What's this?" Mr. Oliver asked about halfway down the bookstore aisle. Lydia almost ran into him when he stopped in his tracks. His foot had crunched on something as he'd taken a step. He bent down to pick up a small piece of metal. "It seems to be the arms of a cross," he said, holding it out for Lydia to see. "That was a charm on one of the necklaces or bracelets we carry. It couldn't have been broken off by accident."

Lydia didn't know what to say.

"Oh, my," Mr. Oliver said, turning to the small checkout counter near the door. The drawer of the cash register was open—and empty.

"Dearest," Mr. Oliver called back to his wife in the gathering room. "It looks like some money has gone missing." He still talked like Eeyore.

Mrs. Oliver stuck her head through the door from the gathering room, her lips formed into a deep frown. "What are you talking about?"

"It looks like we've had a burglary," Mr. Oliver said, his voice totally calm.

Frank followed Mrs. Oliver into the bookstore, and Brenda came over from the corner of the room where she had been sorting books. Lydia stood where she was, at the cash register.

"I found the drawer open and all the cash gone," Mr. Oliver said. His facial expression was the opposite of Mrs. Oliver's. Not that he looked happy, just not panicked.

"Gone?" Mrs. Oliver exclaimed. "There must have been 250 shekels in there!"

"It looks like some jewelry was taken too," Mr. Oliver said.

Frank went over to the outside door and tested it. "It's unlocked. Anyone could have just walked in."

"We always leave it unlocked when the shop is open," Brenda said. "But we usually have someone in here." She turned to the Olivers. "I should have stayed back. I'm so sorry—"

Mrs. Oliver sat down and her words came out in a sort of choking noise. "First bombed, and now robbed?" She put her hands over her face. "Is someone out to get us?"

Lydia squirmed. That's exactly what she was wondering. She and her dad had to get out of there.

Brenda turned to Lydia. "Hey, weren't you in here while we went in the other room?"

Mrs. Oliver glared at Lydia.

Lydia nodded, blushing. "Just for a minute. I didn't see anything fishy." Was Brenda accusing her? Brenda had been alone in the room too. Why wasn't she being questioned?

Mr. Oliver didn't seem to notice the tension. "It wasn't much," he said to his wife. "It would only amount to about sixty dollars. Besides, it's just money."

"True, true," Mrs. Oliver said, standing up and forcing a smile. "It'll take more than that to get us to give up."

She looked directly at Lydia when she said it.

"We have to find that money, Dad," Lydia insisted the moment they got in the cab. They were headed to the Mount of Olives to do some sightseeing.

"The money is gone, Lyd."

"Maybe we can still catch the guy!"

"How do you know it's a guy?" Frank asked.

"I'm just saying, Dad!"

"Just saying what? It's none of our business."

The road ducked into a long, dark tunnel under another road—the perfect place for a suicide bomber to strike.

Lydia harrumphed.

"What?" Frank demanded. "Why the scowl?"

"Dad, Mrs. Oliver thinks I stole the money—and broke the cross jewelry."

"No, she doesn't," Frank said immediately. "Why would she think that?"

"Because I was alone in the room around the time it happened. Brenda thinks I did it too. I can tell."

"Lydia, cross this off your list of things to feel guilty about."

They came up out of the tunnel and Lydia could see the walls of the Old City again—plus trillions of people wandering around buying or selling trinkets in the afternoon heat.

"*I* don't feel guilty, but I don't like someone else thinking I am," Lydia said. "We have to find out who really is guilty."

"No, we don't," Frank said, sounding slightly annoyed. "What we need to do is determine if this city needs any more Jesus freaks."

Lydia couldn't help but laugh. "Jesus freaks? Is that what the Olivers are?"

"That's what we are!"

Lydia remembered the dc Talk song and realized Frank meant that in a positive way. Then she thought the stack of Olivers' books. "Dad, do we really have to believe Jesus is God to get to heaven?"

Frank blinked at her. "Where'd that come from?"

"Huh? Oh, I don't know. Just thinking about that big poster of the Olivers, I guess. And their book: *The Only Way*, or whatever." She shuddered. "It just feels like . . . I don't know . . . like . . . whatever."

Her dad chuckled. "Sounds a bit like a Santa Claus story, doesn't it? 'All you have to do is believe.' Only it's not a Santa story. It's really true."

Typical response. He would never give her a straight answer to something she already knew. It *was* kind of weird to be questioning this stuff. Lydia had been going to church all her life. It was just that she had never really met non-Christian religious people before. Was this Jewish family they were staying with really going down to the devil even though they seemed so good?

"It's not so much unbelievable," Lydia said, "as it is . . . well, mean."

"Yes, it is hard to find that balance between mercy and truth."

"Dad! You're not hearing me. Mrs. Oliver makes Christianity ugly."

"Lydia! You just met Mrs. Oliver—plus her house got bombed. You shouldn't talk about her like that."

"I thought we were here to criticize," Lydia said.

"To *discern*, Peachoo—to see what works and what doesn't."

"Well, I'm pretty sure that what Mrs. Oliver does doesn't work." Lydia was forcing herself not to cry. "And I didn't steal her money!"

She looked up at her dad, hoping for some word of assurance.

She got it. He reached over and patted her arm. "Of course you didn't, honey. I'll stand behind you on that."

The Mount of Olives was so stunning Lydia thought she might quit breathing. She even almost forgot to worry about terrorist attacks.

They were standing at the top of one low mountain looking over a valley toward another mountaintop, Mount Zion, where the Old City was—looking at so many of the places she had read about in the Bible. She could see the Garden of Gethsemane, where Jesus had wept when Judas had been about to betray Him; the place where the Temple had been, now turned into a Muslim mosque called the Dome of the Rock; and the place where they say Jesus was crucified, buried, and resurrected.

From where she was standing, she could practically hit a baseball to each of those places. Or at least someone could—she was a lousy hitter. The point is that when she had read the stories in the Bible, she had imagined these places far apart. Now she could see they were all stuffed together.

Lydia let her eyes linger on the Old City walls, which, even from this distance, looked old but strong. The wind swept up from the garden deep in the valley below her, moving her attention there. The leaves of the olive trees showed silvery green, and dust blew up from the pathways into her eyes and nose.

She couldn't concentrate for long. A man wearing aviator sunglasses tried to get Lydia and her dad to buy a panoramic photo of the view. Then a man in a flowered red shirt tried to get her to pay for a ride on his colorfully decorated camel. Lydia just wanted to be left alone to pray.

Which was kind of weird for her. Good, but weird.

And she did pray. She kept her eyes open and she didn't say "our Father who art in heaven" or even "please save me from raving mad terrorists," but she was most certainly praying—simply letting her heart sing at God's greatness.

"Lydia!" a male voice called from behind her. She didn't recognize the voice. Lydia turned around and saw Marcus, the cute boy from the American tour group.

"Hi, Marcus!" she said, amazed that her voice didn't fail her. "How's the tour?"

"Bor-ing!"

Marcus was wearing cargo pants and a long-sleeved graphic T-shirt, and he was carrying a camera. His hair was less wild today, but those beautiful black eyes were still there—and right now they were looking only at her.

"Boring?" Lydia repeated. "I keep wondering when the next bomb will hit!"

"Yeah, well, that part is fun."

Lydia burst out laughing. "You're crazy! I'm glad we're only here for a week or my nerves would give out."

"Your nerves?" Marcus asked, looking like he wasn't sure if he had heard her right.

Whoops. She was starting to sound like her friend Ben, who always sounded a bit like an old lady even though he was only fourteen. Lydia had definitely been hanging around adults too much. "Whatever," she quickly said. "Do you want to hear the latest Pillar song I downloaded this morning?"

"This morning? You have Internet access?"

She was back in kid territory. Phew. "Yeah, at the place we stayed last night."

"I thought you stayed at the Christian Hope Center with the Olivers. A few of us went over there this morning, but I didn't see you. Actually, I didn't see anyone."

He'd been looking for her? She tried not to look too excited at that little bit of news. She also tried brush away the thought that he, too, had been at the scene of the crime when the money had been stolen, and that maybe he . . .

"No," she said, "we're staying at a Jewish guesthouse in the Jewish Quarter."

"Inside the Old City?"

"Yeah."

"Cool, Lydia. Do you know how old that place is?"

"I know! It's great." She glanced across to the Old City wall and thought of the Bible stories telling how it had been built—and knocked down, and rebuilt. It all happened so long ago, yet it was right here! "So, who all went over to the Christian Hope Center this morning?"

Marcus shifted his feet and mumbled, "Oh, just me and my sister."

He looked uncomfortable, so Lydia quickly changed the subject. If he had been looking for her, she wasn't going to put him on the spot for it. "So, do you want to hear the song? It's awesome!"

Marcus looked around and pointed to a ledge behind a billboard that advertised one of the many tour companies in Jerusalem. "Let's go over there and listen."

Lydia went, of course. Of all the girls on this trip, she was the one he wanted to spend time with. They each put in an earpiece, and they leaned their heads close together as they listened. Lydia hardly heard the song because her heart was thumping so loudly.

"Cool!" Marcus said when the song was over. "Thanks, Lydia!"

They slipped back to the other side of the sign, and Lydia immediately spotted her dad looking around anxiously. His eyes locked on hers for a moment, and then he looked at Marcus, who happened to be pulling Lydia in for a sideways hug.

"Um . . . I gotta go," Lydia said quietly. She started walking toward her dad, who was still staring at Marcus with an I-dare-you-to-speak-to-my-daughter-again look on his face. "See you around."

"Wait!" Marcus called. "Can I have your e-mail address or something?" He obviously hadn't noticed Frank or he would have shut up.

Lydia kept walking. As much as she wanted to stay in touch with Marcus, there was no way she would do anything about it now.

"Who. Was. That." Frank's words came out almost in a whisper, but Lydia felt like he had yelled at her.

"Dad!" she begged. "Don't make a scene!" She glanced at Marcus, who seemed to catch on finally. He disappeared into the crowd.

Frank turned to stare at her. "Don't make a scene? Who made a scene here? Who disappeared from sight only to reappear with a boy—a boy!"

"Da-ad."

"What were you doing behind that billboard?"

"Can you lower your voice, Dad?" Lydia whispered. "We just listened to a song on my iPod. What's the big deal?"

Wrong words. Her dad completely lost it. "The big deal is that my daughter went missing in a dangerous foreign country *by her own choice* and then acts as if being alone with a stranger here is a perfectly acceptable thing!"

"Marcus is not a stranger. We met him at the Olivers' guesthouse last night." She put her arms around her dad's tummy and put her head on his chest. "I'm sorry for scaring you, Daddy. I love you."

Frank stayed tense for a few more seconds, then he sighed and hugged Lydia back. "You just be careful." He held her a moment longer.

Lydia laughed. What else could she do? "Dad, I'm fourteen years old! You act like I'm a little girl."

"You *are* a little girl!" he said, taking her hand in his. "Now come on. Let's go down to the Church of the Agony."

"Ooh! That sounds like fun."

The rest of the morning was spent touring Jerusalem outside the walls of the Old City. But Lydia had her eyes open for just two things: terrorist attacks and sightings of Marcus.

She saw neither.

Frank and Lydia arrived back at Shalom Guesthouse to find that the beds had been made and fresh towels placed on the nightstand. Lydia smiled. Too bad the maid hadn't attacked the pile of clothes she had left in the corner—then life would be perfect. They went down for a quiet lunch in the café, then Frank disappeared upstairs for a nap. "Jet lag," he said, even though it was only a two-hour time change from Liberia. Her dad was definitely getting old.

Lydia went to the computer to see if Ben had e-mailed back. He had.

Lyd im worried bout u. I think u were safer here. We have to talk. When can you IM?

Lydia wrote back.

Tonight. 8pm your time. 10pm my time. If that doesn't work, tomorrow. 6am your time 8am my time. Lots to tell.

She clicked "send," and then felt a hand on her shoulder.

5

Tricked

Y ou must be feeling guilty," Sarah said.

Lydia stared at her. "What are you talking about?"

"You jumped when I touched you," Sarah said as she plopped down on the chair next to Lydia. "Everyone knows that's a sign of guilt." Today Sarah was wearing a white shirt with a black and red tie, and had her hair done in two ponytails.

"It's a sign of being freaked out because someone came creeping up behind me." Actually, Lydia *was* jumpy. She hadn't stopped being on full alert since the bombing the night before. Now she found it hard to relax even in the safety of the Shalom Guesthouse.

"No, I think you jumped because you were writing to your boyfriend again." Sarah grinned. "Or aren't you allowed to have a boyfriend yet?"

Boyfriend? Lydia thought back to how her dad had acted that afternoon when he'd seen her with Marcus. "I don't think I'll be allowed to have a boyfriend until I'm eighty-five. My dad is over the top about things like that."

Sarah groaned. "I know what you mean. My dad would like to lock me in the house."

"Really?" Lydia asked, turning to face Sarah. "Your dad is like that too?"

Sarah laughed and choked and snorted at the same time—sounding something like a horse with its face stuck in a tuba. The two girls howled with laughter at the unexpected noise.

When they finally quit laughing, Lydia said, "You know English well, don't you?"

Sarah's face lit up. "Do you think so? My dad wants me to speak Hebrew at home, but I like being . . . ehr . . . with the times. I watch TV and copy the American accent. It makes him mad."

"I wish I knew another language. I can count in Spanish, but that's about all."

Sarah shrugged. "You're American. Americans never know anything other than English." She leaned forward and whispered, "So, tell the truth. Were you writing to your boyfriend?"

Lydia shook her head. "Ben's just a friend."

Sarah laughed and stood up. "Come on."

"Where?"

"Just come on."

Lydia logged out and followed Sarah up the staircase at the far end of the old house. Whatever Sarah wanted to do *had* to be better than listening to her dad snore.

At the top of the stairs, the landing opened up into a large living room with old-fashioned wallpaper on the walls. Sarah walked through the room, past a tiny kitchen and stuffy dining room, and into what must have been her bedroom. Sarah flopped onto her bed and gestured to the beanbag on the floor.

Lydia looked around Sarah's room. It was full of typical girl stuff—stuffed animals, posters of Orlando Bloom, and shoes—though it was smaller than Lydia's bedroom at home, or what had been her bedroom before they'd sold their house to begin working for GRO. Lydia felt a twinge of homesickness.

"Okay," Sarah whispered loudly, "tell me the truth now. Who's Ben?"

41

Lydia couldn't help laughing. "You're obsessed with this. He really is just a friend." Sarah looked at her doubtfully and Lydia sat down in the beanbag chair. "Fine. Maybe this will help you believe me. Ben is a geeky thirteen-year-old who is shorter than me." She held out her hands as if to say, "Need I say more?"

"Oh." Sarah sounded disappointed. "Well, do you have a boyfriend?"

Lydia shook her head. "Not really. I sort of like this kid named Marcus though. I've only met him a couple of times, but today we listened to some music together."

Sarah leaned forward. "He's here?"

"Yeah, he's staying at Novotel. He's American too. I met him at the other—"

"Did you hold hands?"

Lydia rolled her eyes. "No!"

"Have you ever held hands with a boy?"

Sarah looked at her so intently that Lydia couldn't help laughing. And once she got started she couldn't quit. She grabbed her stomach and fell off the beanbag, tears streaming down her cheeks.

"I'll take that as a no," Sarah said.

Lydia tried to compose herself. "I'm sorry. I'm not laughing at you. It just struck me as funny."

Sarah waited, her thin, perfectly plucked eyebrows raised.

"The answer is no," Lydia said, still giggling. "I've never held hands with a boy."

Sarah softened. "Me neither. My dad would kill me if he knew I even thought about it."

"I'm surprised my dad hasn't invented some contraption that blocks my mind from thinking certain things."

"You mean like the computer programs that block certain Internet pages?" Sarah laughed. "My dad would buy stock in that."

"Can rabbis by stocks?"

"What?"

"Isn't your dad a rabbi?"

This time Sarah laughed. "Are you kidding? He's a business-man—and he's big into politics. He'd be a lousy rabbi. My uncle's a rabbi, though. I wish he were my dad."

Lydia had never heard anyone say out loud that they wanted to exchange their parents—even though every kid she knew could point out twenty major flaws in their parents in 2.5 seconds flat. "You're terrible!" she said, grinning. "Talking about your dad that way."

"Are you kidding?" Sarah said. "My dad is crazy. He's too mean to me, and too nice to everyone else."

"How about your mom?" Lydia asked—but she immediately regretted it, because she didn't want Sarah asking the same question back. Lydia's mom had died when Lydia was six.

Sarah shrugged. "She's alright, I guess. Just boring." She got up off the bed. "Let's go."

"Where?"

"Out."

"Alright, but I'd better go tell my dad."

Sarah whipped around to stare at Lydia. "*What?* We can't tell our parents!"

"Why not? It's not like we're doing anything wrong." Lydia wondered if this little outing was a good idea. "Are we?"

"I told you how strict my dad was, didn't I? It wouldn't matter if it was wrong or not, he'd still say no."

"If it's not wrong, why would he say no? My dad wouldn't."

"Yes, he would."

"I'd bet you anything he wouldn't," Lydia said. Her dad would probably be glad she was making a friend.

Sarah's face lit up. "Really? You'll bet on that?"

Lydia shrugged. This girl was crazy. "It's just a saying."

"No way. You said you'd bet. Do you have any money?"

"Some." Her dad always gave her a little bit to carry around for emergencies. She didn't think this would qualify. Right now she had forty shekels in her pocket, which was not quite ten dollars, plus some American coins. "I'll bet you a dollar."

"I don't have American money," Sarah said. She stuck out her hand to shake. "I'll bet you a hundred shekels."

"Too much." That was like twenty-five dollars.

Sarah held her hand out even more firmly. "If you know you're right, why worry?"

As the girls shook hands, Lydia almost hoped her dad *would* refuse to let her go. It was hard to turn Sarah down, and who knew what kind of trouble she would get them in?

Frank was in the lobby chatting with some Jewish men. Apparently his "jet lag" hadn't done him in for too long.

Lydia had made introductions and Sarah quickly went in for the kill. "Would you be comfortable with Lydia joining me off campus for a little while?" As if they were even on campus. Lydia almost rolled her eyes.

"Where is it you want to go?" Frank asked Sarah.

"To visit a friend, sir," Sarah said. She smiled. "It's not far. Lydia will be perfectly safe."

The "sir" worked. Frank smiled. And in the smile Lydia knew she was going to win the bet. She wasn't sure how she felt about that—but a hundred shekels had to be good, right?

"Sounds like a good opportunity for you to make some friends, Lydia," he said. "Have fun. Be careful."

"It's not like you earned it," Sarah said sourly. She counted out the money into Lydia's hand, out of earshot of her dad. "He would have said no if I hadn't talked him into it."

"Fine. Don't pay."

Sarah stared at her. "Are you joking? We made a bet."

"Okay," Lydia said with a shrug. "Then pay." She still felt weird about taking Sarah's money, but there seemed to be no way out of it.

Lydia stuffed the money into the front pocket of her jeans and followed her new friend out the door of the guesthouse. It wouldn't be dark for another couple hours, but the narrow streets, dark alcoves, and crooked alleys seemed tailor-made for thieves.

Sarah giggled. "I've never made a bet before. My dad would kill me if he knew."

"Really?"

"Yes." Sarah turned to Lydia and grabbed her arm. "So do *not* tell anyone. Please!"

Lydia shrugged again. "Okay."

"Thanks. Let's go."

"Where are we going?"

Sarah smiled. "You'll see."

About ten minutes after leaving the Old City—which wasn't just around the corner, as Sarah had promised—the girls walked up to Novotel, a large, ultramodern hotel. This was where Marcus was staying. Lydia wanted to scream. Or cry. Why had she trusted this girl? Her dad would kill her for coming here.

45

Lydia heard voices and turned around to see the whole gang of Americans she had met at the Olivers' guesthouse walking into the hotel.

She scanned the group for Marcus, but didn't see him. She did spot the girl who had made fun of Mrs. Oliver the night of the bombing. Lydia knew the girl had to be in high school to join Youth Around the World, but she looked like she was in college. It's not that she was tall—in fact, she was shorter than Lydia—but she had an expression that made her seem old, like she knew it all. She was slender, wore very tight clothes, and her curly black hair was pulled into an elegant bun with just one or two curls left along her face. Lydia knew this girl would have been one of the snobby kids in her school, yet Lydia couldn't help wanting to impress her. Lydia quickly smoothed her hair and wondered why in the world Sarah hadn't told her where they were going.

"Lydia?" the girl said. "Is that you?"

Lydia couldn't believe the girl remembered her name, but Sarah walked right up and stuck out her hand. "Yes, and I'm Sarah."

By now the whole gang had walked up to them, including Dr. Erwin, the cool Bible teacher who had been making jokes with Lydia's dad. Today she was wearing jeans and a few layers of V-neck shirts with a big colorful necklace.

They moved under the hotel's awning to allow the valets help some people out of a car.

"What are you doing here?" the girl asked Lydia.

Sarah said nothing, but looked at Lydia.

"Umm," Lydia said, wishing she had the guts to blame it on Sarah. "Brenda told me you were here, and I just wanted to see if everyone was alright." That *was* true.

"Fortunately, yes," Dr. Erwin said, "though some of us have seen better days." She pointed to a boy whose arm was in a cast, and Lydia remembered with a shock that he was the one she had helped. "But we're all alive. Thank the Lord! How's your father?"

Lydia trembled a little bit as the memory of that horrid evening washed over her.

Dr. Erwin stepped forward. "Lydia? Is he okay?"

Lydia nodded and wished she could sit down. "Yeah. He's fine. He didn't get hurt at all."

"Is he here too?" Dr. Erwin asked, looking around.

"No, just Sarah and me." She gestured with little enthusiasm toward her new friend. She really, *really* wished they hadn't come here. "I guess we should be heading back now."

Dr. Erwin looked intently at Lydia. "Does your dad know you're here?"

"Of course he does," Sarah said confidently. "He sent us."

Lydia was wondering what to do about this huge lie when she heard a familiar voice behind her. "Why don't you stay and hang out for a while?"

It was Marcus. He stepped up beside her. Lydia's insides flipped like a dolphin at Sea World.

She noticed the pretty girl shoot a look at Marcus and then start grinning, but Marcus didn't seem to notice.

"Umm, sure," Lydia said, suddenly not minding so much that Sarah had tricked her. "We can stay a *little* while."

6

To Enemy Territory

The lobby of the Novotel was huge, with lots of tables and couches. Just like the outside, the inside could have passed for any hotel in America except that there were more Jewish people wearing skullcaps than back home. Someone handed Lydia a Coke, and the grown-ups wandered to another part of the lobby. Sarah quickly made friends with everyone and kept bragging about what good friends she and Lydia were. Marcus was cracking everyone up with his jokes. And even the pretty girl, whose name was Michelle, turned out to be pretty cool.

"You like my brother, don't you?" Michelle whispered to Lydia.

"Your brother?"

"Marcus," Michelle said, discreetly nodding toward him.

"Oh! He's your brother." Lydia hoped she didn't look too relieved. "I thought maybe you liked him."

Michelle threw her head back and laughed loudly. "That dope! Are you kidding?" Then she squeezed Lydia's hand.

"I can't believe you and Sarah went out exploring on your own," Michelle said. "I haven't been able to step out of sight of our teachers since the bombing. Well, except once." She smiled mysteriously and leaned closer to Lydia. "You seem cool, and I can tell *you* this," she whispered. "But I could get in lots of trouble if anyone found out. Promise not to tell anyone?"

Lydia didn't want to hear it. She was starting to feel more and more guilty about being there. Her dad thought she was somewhere else, *with* someone else. The last thing she wanted was another secret. Lydia was relieved when Marcus cut into the conversation.

"Hey," he said, grabbing Lydia's arm, "did you hear who bombed the guesthouse?"

"No!" Lydia said, trying to ignore the tingling she felt at being so close to Marcus. "Did they find out?"

"They were saying on TV that an unnamed American teenager, a guest of the Olivers', was responsible," Marcus said, laughing.

Lydia's gut did another flip, but this time it didn't feel like a frolicking dolphin—it was more like a shark hunting prey. The people on TV were blaming someone in her group? Did they think it was *her*?

"Marcus!" Michelle snapped. "Don't spread that rumor. It's awful. Of course it wasn't one of us." She turned to Lydia. "Almost right away they found out it was the Arabs."

"That reminds me," Marcus said. "Are you guys going to the West Bank at all? We're going to Bethlehem!"

Sarah looked horrified. "You shouldn't go there. It's dangerous!"

"I know," Marcus said, gleefully. "I can't wait!"

Lydia refocused. Marcus's words seemed wrong. She couldn't believe he wasn't the least bit afraid, after what he'd been through at the guesthouse. Maybe he was bluffing to show off for her. She couldn't help smiling.

"That's where all the terrorists live," Sarah said.

"It'll be cool!" Marcus said. He picked up an imaginary pistol and started acting like a secret spy, peeking around some make-believe corner.

"Well, I don't want to go there," Lydia said. Who'd want to go near people who could bomb a Christian guesthouse?

Sarah leaned close to Lydia's ear. "I think we should get going."

Lydia looked at her watch. It was already six o'clock. They'd been there an hour or so, but it had felt like only five minutes. She stood up. "Guys, we need to go now."

They groaned. "Can't you stay?" Michelle asked.

"No, not this time."

"It was great to see all of you," Lydia said. She couldn't help looking at Marcus when she said that.

He jumped up. "Hey, what's your e-mail address?"

Lydia gave it to him—plus her IM screen name.

"I might not be able to write right away," he said. "My dad said part of this trip is to get me to 'disconnect'—to quit being so hooked on electronics, or something like that."

"Oh." Lydia didn't know what to say.

"But what my parents don't know won't hurt them," Marcus said. Then he winked. "I'll write you."

Lydia almost died. She wished her best friend Amy were there so they could scream together the second Marcus was out of earshot. Instead, she linked arms with Sarah and calmly walked outside.

Lydia's giddiness disappeared almost immediately. She would have to tell her dad where they had gone. And she wouldn't be able to blame this on Sarah—her dad would just say, "You could have turned around." And he'd be right.

They walked for a few minutes in silence. Lydia noticed that the sun was lower, but she was glad it wasn't dark yet.

"Don't listen to that boyfriend of yours," Sarah finally said. "The West Bank would not be fun. Even here you've got to keep your eyes open for . . . ehr . . . terrorists."

"How do you spot them?" Lydia asked.

"They're Palestinians," Sarah said in the same tone of voice she would have said, "Duh."

"All Palestinians are terrorists?" Lydia asked. She could just imagine what her dad would say to that. He couldn't stand stereotypes. One time Lydia had made the mistake of saying "Boys are dumb," and he'd lectured her for a half hour about racism—of all things. He had prattled on about how "that kind of thinking" leads to a "false superior attitude" that ends up "breaking down every relationship."

Since then Lydia hadn't shown off her Happy Bunny T-shirts to him very often.

"Of course they are," Sarah said. "All Palestinians are dangerous."

They walked on, arms still linked. Lydia tried to spot terrorists in the busy crowds, but the only Palestinians she could see looked like normal people dressed for work.

"Christians aren't as bad as I thought," Sarah said a moment later.

Lydia laughed. "What's that supposed to mean?"

"None of you guys tried to convert me or anything," Sarah said. "I hate missionaries."

Lydia thought of Mrs. Oliver and how offensive she would be to Sarah.

"You guys *are* Christians, right?" Sarah asked.

"Yeah, of course!" Lydia said, a bit offended. She let go of Sarah's arm. "My dad's a—" She stopped herself.

"What?" Sarah asked.

Lydia could see the gate to the Old City and started walking faster. "He's a development worker."

Sarah walked faster too. "A development worker? What's that got to do with being Christian?"

Lydia sighed and wondered how she'd gotten herself into this. "He's a missionary, okay?"

Sarah's eyes got big. "Like the people who own the guest-house that was bombed?"

Lydia kept walking. "Well . . ."

"Why would you want to be like them?"

A cab pulled up beside them and the driver asked if they wanted a ride. Lydia said no, but the man continued to drive slowly beside them, saying he would give them a good deal.

Finally Sarah turned to him, tossed her head, and said something in Hebrew. She sounded mad. The man grumbled something back and drove off. By this time they were at the gate, and Lydia was once again bombarded by people trying to sell her stuff. Everyone seemed to think she needed new jewelry or postcards or something. Lydia ignored them.

"Seriously," Sarah said when they'd finally gotten away from the hawkers, "do you really think that Jesus dude was God?"

Lydia could feel her annoyance flare into anger. She tried not to show it, but she wasn't very successful. "Yes, I do, Sarah. But that doesn't mean I'm like Mrs. Oliver."

Thankfully, they had arrived at the Shalom Guesthouse. Lydia turned to walk inside, but Sarah pulled on her arm. "But He died, Lydia. Jesus died. Why would God let his Son die?" Her eyes flitted back and forth over Lydia's.

Lydia didn't know what to say. She knew the right answers—they were in her head somewhere. She'd think of them later and kick herself for not remembering. But right now her brain was as blank as the stone walls of the Old City.

Sarah let go of Lydia's arm, disgust in her eyes. "And why in the world would you come to Israel to try to teach that garbage to Jewish people? Why can't people just leave us alone?"

Sarah stormed into the guesthouse.

"Oh, good," Frank said. Lydia had just walked in to the lobby behind Sarah. Lydia's dad was sitting in a chair reading the paper. "You're back. I was just starting to get worried."

Lydia wondered what she should tell him first—that she just had a fight with Sarah or that they had gone to Novotel. "Dad," she said, looking down.

"Wait a sec." He called out to Sarah just as she was about to disappear into her family's rooms. "Hey, Sarah!" As usual, he was clueless when it came to reading other people's emotions. When Sarah turned to look at him he said, "Did you have nice time?"

"Sure," Sarah said, turning to walk again.

"You and Lydia had better exchange e-mail addresses or something," he said, folding his newspaper and standing up. "We're getting ready to head out."

Sarah waved a very unconcerned good-bye and closed the door behind her.

"What!" Lydia said. "We just got here."

"Mr. Klein was nice enough to let us stay for one night," Frank said. "I don't want to overstay our welcome." He looked toward where Sarah had been and said, "Maybe we already have." He must have picked up a clue after all.

"Where are we going?"

"Uh," Frank said. He shrugged his shoulders and put his fingers in his hair—a sure sign that he was up to something. "I got us a hotel. A very nice one."

Lydia wasn't falling for it. "Where are we going, Dad?"

"Nothing to worry about," he said, much too casually. "We're just going to Bethlehem."

"Bethlehem!" Lydia said. "Isn't that in Palestinian territory?" Her heart felt like it had just jumped on a trampoline and got stuck in the back of her throat. "That's where all the terrorists are!"

Frank chuckled. "We'll see about that." He put his arm around her shoulders and led her to their room. "Come on, let's pack and then go out to eat."

✝ ✝ ✝

They left for the West Bank shortly after dinner. Although Bethlehem is just a couple of miles from Jerusalem, the ride there took over twenty minutes. The cab driver took them the long way around. "We go through Beit Jalla so we don't need to go through the checkpoint," he said.

It sounded suspicious to Lydia. She held on to the door handle just in case they needed to bolt.

Once they crossed into the West Bank, the neighborhood changed from having mostly Jewish people on the street to having none at all. It was dark by now, though, and people seemed to have gone indoors. Those she did see were Arabs, mostly teenagers, wearing American jeans and T-shirts. In some doorways, groups of two or three men sat smoking cigarettes and talking quietly.

The Nativity Hotel looked nice enough. It was small and neat. The hotel manager, a tall clean-shaven Palestinian man with a huge smile, was very friendly and seemed glad to have them there . . . but Lydia knew he was a possible terrorist. He chatted for a long time before giving them keys to their suite, asking all kinds of questions about where they were from and how they liked the Holy Land.

"Time for bed, kid," Frank said when they finally settled in. "We have to leave early tomorrow for the tour." They were taking

54

a day trip in the hills of the Galilee, in the footsteps of Jesus. "It's already ten o'clock."

"It is?" That's what time she was supposed to meet Ben online. "Can I go online first?" Their host had showed them where there was a computer with free Internet access. "I have to talk to Ben."

Frank sighed. "Fine. Make it quick."

Ben wasn't online and he hadn't sent an e-mail.

Lydia set her alarm for 5:59 a.m. The next morning she went down to the computer—still wearing her pajamas—but Ben still wasn't online. Lydia hoped everything was alright.

Her dad woke up a few minutes after Lydia got back to the suite. "Good morning, Peachoo. That's unusual—up before your dad." He shrugged. "Let's go get some grub."

As soon as Lydia stuffed the food down her throat—cucumbers, tomatoes, and eggs—she ran off to take a shower. Ever since she had left Liberia, where hot and cold running water are a luxury, she was back to showering everyday and wearing more stylish clothes. Surely that had nothing to do with the fact that she was hoping to bump into a particular fifteen-year-old American tourist.

7

Forever at Odds

We are not terrorists!" Mohammed yelled. He hit the steering wheel of the little Chevy Aveo he used as a taxi. It sent them veering off the two-lane highway onto the shoulder, where the car sent up a cloud of dust. He righted their path and sped along the road into the desolate hills.

In the backseat Lydia gripped the armrest, trying to send her dad a telepathic message to jump out of the car at the next opportunity. But Frank sat calmly in the front seat nodding his head like the bobble-head doll on the dashboard.

"It is all the fault of the media!" the wild man who was serving as their tour guide said in heavily accented English as he nearly plunged them into the ditch on the other side of the road. "TV reporters want good story. They want blame somebody," the man nearly shouted, "and they choose *Ahrrr*abs." Mohammed rolled his r's so thickly that Lydia had trouble understanding that he meant *Arabs*.

Frank shook his head sadly, as if the guy had said his dog just died.

"You think I am angry?" Mohammed asked. "Our land was taken! Yes, I am angry!"

Frank added an exclamation point with a sharp nod of his head.

"Am I angry that our land, the West Bank, has been occupied by foreigners for more than forty years? Am I angry that our people live as prisoners in their own cities? Yes!"

Frank jabbed his head forward.

"Am I angry that I cannot entry the Holy City without showing identity card and being questioned by armed guards? And that my brother cannot even ride in my taxi because he do not have right kind of permit? That my mother cannot enter Jerusalem to visit my sick child in hospital? Yes, I am angry! But I am no terrorist. Never!"

Frank turned to look at the man Lydia was pretty sure really was a terrorist, and his face got all soft. "I'm sorry, brother."

Lydia felt her eyes nearly pop out of her head. Grandmothers not being able to see sick kids is sad and all that, but she and her dad were likely to die at this man's hands any minute. That was even sadder! This guy was a Muslim radical, probably one of those people who bombed the Olivers' guesthouse, and there sat her dad in the front seat of the car, chatting for the last hour as if they were best friends.

"You've got a sick baby?" Frank asked.

Lydia could hardly believe it when Mohammed thrust his sleeve up to his face and wiped away a tear. "I think my young son is not so strong to stay with us."

"That's harsh," Frank said. Both men were quiet, and Lydia, for just a second, felt sorry for him. "What's the matter with your son?"

"He was born with, uh . . . " He thumped his chest in a quick rhythm. "Ah . . . not right with his . . . Bump-bump, bump-bump."

Frank nodded. "Something wrong with his heart?"

"Yes! Heart defect." Mohammed sniffed and looked away. "That is no surprise. The hearts of all our people is broken. It is no time for a Palestinian to enter the world."

They drove in silence. Mohammed seemed to gained control of his car again.

"Look there," he said, pointing up the hill beside the road. "That is settlement." A cement fence topped by razor wire separated the barren land from a green neighborhood; new homes made of the traditional white stone of the land were scattered along well-kept streets that circled through the neighborhood.

"A settlement?" Frank asked.

"Israeli settlement. On our land. Palestinian land. But the Israelis, they take it over. They move in and build houses—for Israeli only, not Palestinian."

"You see," Mohammed said, "they are afraid of us, so they put up big fences to keep us out. And they put checkpoints on road so we cannot travel to other towns."

Sure enough, the vehicle approached a barricade in the road, manned by a team of Israeli soldiers. A little pole blocked the road, but a huge armored tank watched over the scene from a few yards away.

Mohammed slowed the car down, but he spoke quickly. "Passports. Get passports ready. Open windows and glove box. Keep hands in sight and say nothing." He stopped beside a little booth where men and women, dressed in green military fatigues and berets, waited with their hands on their rifles. One of the guards stood at the narrow space they would have to drive through with his gun pointed right at them. He held up his hand and glared at Mohammed as if he had just been arrested for some terrible crime.

Mohammed held up his identity card as though it were a bulletproof vest and slowly exited the car. Two soldiers searched his body, looked through the trunk, and drilled him with questions.

Another soldier came to Frank's window and demanded his passport, which he looked at carefully while keeping one hand on his rifle. He looked at the passport photo, then eyed Frank thoroughly. Then he did the same for Lydia. The soldier looked to be around twenty or so, and Lydia would have thought he was cute if he hadn't looked so mean.

"Go on," he said a few moments later. "Get out of here."

Mohammed was trembling when he got back in the car.

A mile past the checkpoint he spoke again. "I will tell you a story. It is a story I heard as a small boy, and a story I tell to my children. It is a story that tells why can be no peace between my people and the Israelis."

Mohammed didn't say anything for a while longer, but Lydia didn't lose interest. She watched the countryside go slowly by, staring at the Jordan River down the hill to the right. It looked like a small creek, and the green plants on either side of it contrasted the brown hills. This was one of the places Jesus must have walked, and He must have hung out with people like Mohammed.

"One day a man wanted to enjoy his beautiful country, so he packed picnic and walked up hill to have a meal under olive tree."

Lydia could see several olive trees atop a hill on the left side of the car. They were short trees, and their branches spread wide. They looked a bit like apple trees back home, but with pretty, silvery green leaves.

"When the man got to hilltop and took his food, he saw giant snake coming toward him," Mohammed said. "The man was afraid—who would not be afraid of such a creature? Quickly he threw bread and cheese to the snake—and the beast ate it!"

Mohammed looked back at Lydia to be sure she was listening. He smiled a little when he saw she was sitting forward in her seat.

"In return," Mohammed continued, "snake opened its mouth, and out came a bright jewel. Every day the man went up hill and to offer bread and cheese to the snake. Every day the snake ate food and offered jewel in return. The man became very rich and very happy."

Lydia looked toward the Jordan River on her right where the sun was halfway to its noon position.

"One day, however, man decided to make hajj."

"Hajj?" Lydia frowned.

"It's a pilgrimage," Frank explained. "Muslims are supposed to make a pilgrimage to Mecca during their lifetime."

Mohammed continued. "Before he left, the man said to his son, 'My son, you must go to hilltop to eat your meal each day. There you meet mighty snake, but do not be afraid. Give snake your bread and cheese, and it will give a jewel.'

"The son did as he was told first day and second day and third day. And he marveled at the precious jewels. But on fourth day, the boy said to himself, 'Why do I wait every day for jewel when I can take it all now?' So when the giant snake went to eat food, the boy swung his knife to kill it."

Lydia winced.

"But the snake turned," Mohammed said, and the knife struck its tail. Quickly the snake lashed out and bit the boy, killing him."

Lydia's eyes were wide. "What happened next? Did the man ever come back?"

Mohammed paused. "Yes," he said slowly. "The man returned to the hilltop. Once again he offered bread and cheese to the snake. But the snake refused to accept the gift, moving aside to show the mane the body of his dead son. 'I cannot accept your gift,' the snake said. 'Your son has wounded me, and I have killed him. Never will we forget this. Never will there be peace between us.'"

Mohammed paused, and Lydia waited for the explanation.

"And so it is between the Jews and us Arabs. They have taken our land. They have killed our sons. Never will we forget this. Never will there be peace."

8
Friends with Enemies

The first place Mohammed took Lydia and her dad was not to his secret den packed with weapons of mass destruction, but to the town of Nazareth. Here Jesus had worked as a carpenter with Joseph. It was a small town with many small shops along the main street, which led up a steep hill. Villagers and tourists could be found in equal number, the villagers mostly working in the shops or sitting at street-side cafés, the tourists walking along the street wearing hats and sunglasses. Lydia was surprised at how touristy the town looked. She had expected Nazareth to be quaint.

Mohammed stayed in the car while Lydia and Frank strolled along the street and bought postcards and some food that looked like pizza but tasted like sour pita bread.

At the end of the street was the Church of the Annunciation, which was supposed to be the place where an angel announced to Mary that she would become the mother of Jesus. It was large stone building with steep rock steps leading to it. Lydia ran to the top of the steps and laughed at her dad when he reached her a few minutes later, panting.

They walked hand in hand around the sanctuary, admiring the many pieces of art displayed on the cool stone walls. Each painting was a picture of Mary that had been donated by Christians in a different country. Lydia was proud to see that the American version was the coolest of all—a modern metallic model in front of a swirl of colors. Frank liked the Japanese version the best, but what did dads know about cool?

Next they went to Joseph's church, which was a much smaller stone building next door. What Lydia loved most going down into a cave under the church where they saw the ancient stone that marked the spot where legend says the holy family lived. It was wet and cool and strangely mysterious.

"Have you been there before?" Lydia asked Mohammed when she and her dad got back into the car. She wasn't nearly so scared of their guide now that he had a cold bottle of Coke ready for her. Mohammed started the car and began driving out of Nazareth to the east.

"Yes, it is powerful," he said. "Jesus was great man."

"Huh?" Lydia blurted, squirting Coke through her nose. "I mean, I didn't know you were a Christian."

Mohammed laughed. "Christians and Muslims are more alike than you think," he told her. "We admire Jesus too. He was great prophet."

Lydia looked at her dad. Could this be true?

"Yes, we do have a lot in common," Frank said. "And we Christians could learn some things from our Muslim friends. Their dedication to prayer is something we Christians often lack."

Lydia's mouth was hanging open now. Was her dad actually *praising* Muslims?

Frank went on. "The difference, of course, is that we believe Jesus is more than a great man and a prophet. We believe he is the Son of God. That's what causes all the tension." Frank smiled at their new friend so kindly that it would've been all but impossible for anyone to take offense.

Even so, Mohammed looked startled. "Son of God?" He shook his head a little. "Son of God? Is that what you Christians believe? No wonder you all come here."

Now Frank looked surprised. "You didn't know that?"

Mohammed started up the car, and an embarrassed smile slunk onto his face. "I'm not very religious. I know what I learned in school, but you see no calluses here." He pointed to his forehead.

Lydia looked at her dad for an explanation.

"He means that he does not pray very often. Remember, Muslims bow to touch their foreheads on the ground when they pray—what is it, seven times a day?" he asked Mohammed.

"It is five times," Mohammed said. "If he is devout."

They drove in silence.

"I am sorry," Mohammed finally said, "but I must ask. You believe God could have a son? And if so, would not the son also be God?"

Frank nodded.

"And you believe God could die? Forgive me, but it seems very strange."

Frank settled into his seat. Now it was his turn to tell a story loaded with meaning, and he began slowly, telling the story of Jesus—how he came down from heaven as a helpless baby, "just like us," Frank said, and then lived a perfect, innocent life, so that when he died on the Cross he could take the punishment for all of our sins.

Mohammed nodded slowly as he listened, keeping his eyes on the road. Frank continued the story, explaining that Jesus rose from the dead, and now all we have to do is ask Jesus to forgive our sins and we will be forgiven and will someday join Jesus in heaven, just as he came to earth to be with us.

Mohammed remained silent, but his eyes flicked often toward Frank, so Lydia knew he was listening.

When they arrived at their next stop—the place where Jesus gave the Sermon on the Mount and turned a few pieces of fish and bread into a feast for thousands—Mohammed got out too. "Perhaps I go with you," he said.

This chapel was much smaller than the others, with simple arched doorways opening into a wide, sanctuary that had a mosaic on the floor that formed a picture of loaves and fishes like the ones Jesus multiplied. The few people inside were quietly praying rather than taking pictures and buying trinkets like they had been in most of the other places they had toured so far. Mohammed stood in the back of the room while Frank walked to the front to kneel at the rock where they say Jesus prayed over the fish and bread.

On a whim, Lydia took Mohammed's hand and gently pulled him forward. He smiled and went along. They knelt beside Frank, and the next time Lydia looked at Mohammed, he was crying.

The rest of that day was wild. Lydia had no idea she could have so much fun touring around with two old men. She completely forgot to keep on the lookout for terrorists—or even for Marcus's group. When they were at the Sea of Galilee—where Jesus called the first disciples, and where he calmed the storm and walked on water—Mohammed brought them to a beachfront restaurant where they each ate a huge fish with the head and tail still on it.

"Stay here," Mohammed said to Lydia when the fish arrived. He went to the table beside them on the other side of the white glass, where Lydia could see the shadow of his profile. "Are you watching?" he called.

"What are you doing?" Lydia called back, laughing. She didn't even care that other people in the restaurant were watching too. Mohammed was funny.

Mohammed's shadow held the fish up by its tail and put the whole thing—head first—into his mouth until it disappeared.

Lydia squealed, "Gross!" and quickly leaned over to see how he had pulled off his trick.

"Do not look, child," Mohammed said good-naturedly, and moved back to their table, fish in hand. Apparently he had just moved the fish beside his face and not really into his mouth.

"That was masterful," Frank said. "I'll have to remember that one."

"My children beg me to play that game each time we come here," Mohammed said, chuckling.

After lunch, the three of them went down to the beach beside the Sea of Galilee. It was only about sixty-five degrees, but the sun was shining, and there was hardly any wind. Frank took off his shoes and pretended to walk on the water—only he slipped on a wet stone and got his clothes all wet. Lydia almost laughed so hard it sounded like she was choking. Tears ran down her cheeks.

With teeth chattering, Frank insisted they continue the tour. Next they visited Capernaum, the hometown of Simon Peter. They visited the ruins of what many people think was the home of Simon Peter's mother-in-law. Some say it was the site of the very first Christian church. After that, they visited the nearby Jordan River, in which Jesus was baptized.

"I thought really that happened a long way from here," Lydia said. "Closer to Jerusalem."

"Yes," Mohammed grinned. "But you see, at this place it is much easier for the tour busses to turn around." He winked at Lydia.

Finally it was time to begin the hour-long drive back to Bethlehem. Lydia dozed in the backseat while the men chatted up front.

"It was interesting day with you, for certain," Lydia caught Mohammed saying at one point. "But don't think you make me Christian."

"I make no assumptions about the faith of others," Frank said quietly.

"Muslims don't just become Christian," Mohammed said, as if trying to convince Frank of something. "There are . . . penalties. And remember, I am not religious man."

Sure, Lydia thought, as she drifted back to sleep. That experience in the chapel was most definitely religious. The guy must be in denial.

She woke up a couple times at checkpoints. Once she almost jumped in her seat when a soldier waved an M16 at her. Then the rifle went away, and through the window came the face an Israeli soldier, who winked at her. But after every checkpoint, she fell right back to sleep again. She had all but forgotten that she had nearly been killed by a bomb blast only two days before.

9
Disappointed

"A re you too tired to go out tonight, Lyd?" Frank asked. They were back in their suite at the Nativity Hotel and had changed clothes.

"Of course not. Where are we going?"

"To the Lighthouse—an outreach ministry right here in Bethlehem. I have an appointment with the director. We can walk over after dinner."

"Cool."

Lydia went into her room and dug in a pile of clothes for a hoody. It got chilly at night—though nothing compared to December in Indianapolis. Her fluffy jacket, of course, was gone forever, left at the scene of the bombing on their first night here. She pulled out the money she'd gotten from Sarah and began rummaging around in her suitcase looking for her wallet.

There was a knock. "Come on, Peachoo."

She dropped the cash on the dresser and ran out the door.

Lydia and her dad ate dinner at a small restaurant around the corner from the hotel. They each had a tuna fish sandwich and a huge lettuce salad with some sort of sweet spice in it plus lots of cucumbers. "They serve salad at every meal here," Lydia commented. "I never knew I liked vegetables so much."

"Weird," said Frank.

After dinner they walked about three minutes to the Lighthouse, and the person Frank was meeting hadn't arrived yet. They wandered around a bit, admiring the old stone buildings. The neighborhood seemed all closed up and the streets nearly deserted. Lydia took her dad's arm as they walked. "Um, Dad," she said, suddenly remembering that she hadn't mentioned going to the Novotel with Sarah.

"Yeah, Peachoo?" He kept walking slowly around block they were circling. The Lighthouse building was the largest one in sight, a warehouse surrounded by rectangular white stones. Behind it was something seldom seen in the Holy Lands—grass. A small playground, surrounded by a metal fence, suggested that there were children somewhere in the neighborhood.

"Ummm . . . " How would she say this? "I forgot to tell you that Sarah and I went to the Novotel the other night."

He looked at her blankly.

"That's the hotel where the American tour group is staying."

He wasn't mad. Yet. *Give it time,* Lydia thought. *He'll blow any minute.*

"You mean last night?" Frank asked. "You told me you were going to visit Sarah's friend." Actually, it was Sarah who had said it. Did that make a difference?

"I thought we were too," Lydia said. "But then she took me to Novotel instead." She could see her dad's eyes narrow, so she continued quickly. "Once I got there, I should have turned around, but I didn't. When I saw the other Americans I just . . . stayed." She felt miserable. "I'm sorry." She really was. As much fun as it had been to see Marcus, it was awful to disappoint her dad.

"Well, I guess that means you're going to have to lose a privilege," he said quietly. "You'll be grounded from the computer for a week when we get home."

"But, Dad! We'll only be home two weeks! I want to see—"

"And I do thank you for telling me," he said and kissed her on the head. "I would have had to ground you for the whole time if you hadn't fessed up."

Lydia couldn't believe it. If this was a reward, she would never "fess up" again.

"Well, we may as well head back to the hotel," Frank said. They were nearly to the front of the Lighthouse building. "I don't think they're going to show."

Just then, a small black car squealed into the parking lot and six young adults jumped out, laughing and carrying on.

"Hey!" a young Palestinian guy yelled out to Frank with a friendly wave. He was wearing black slacks with creases down the front, a light-blue shirt, and a graphic yellow tie. He reminded Lydia of Vince Vaughn in nice clothes. "You are Frank Barnes?" His Arabic accent sounded like Mohammed's.

Lydia's dad smiled and walked over with hand outstretched. "Sure am."

The guy shook Frank's hand. "Jordan," he said, then pulled Frank into a very macho hug—like they were sports stars or something. "And this is *Lee*-dia?" He turned to Lydia and she prepared herself for an embrace. The guy didn't hug her, though; he just shook her hand roughly, as if she were part of the gang. "Please, come in," he said, pulling a key out from under the rug by the front door.

The others, who seemed to be of various nationalities, were still laughing and shoving each other by the car, but they all crowded around to say hello to the guests too.

"It's cool you're here, man," an American guy said as he shook Frank's hand. He reminded Lydia of the pictures she'd seen of Jesus, with long hair, a beard, and sandals.

A twenty-something girl with blonde dreadlocks smiled and pulled her cardigan around her shoulders as she stepped next to

Lydia. It was a pretty sweater—long, crocheted, and tied in the front. "Here there are too many fellows," she said quietly to Lydia with a little grin. She had a lovely, romantic accent that Lydia thought must be French. "We two will stick together, no?"

These folks, even Jordan in his professional clothes, were what her dad would call "granola people": They were probably all vegetarians who recycled all their bottles and cans and wore T-shirts saying "Save the Polar Bears"—when they weren't out doing good in underprivileged countries, of course. Lydia liked them much better than the Olivers, and she could see that her dad fit right in with the gang, even if he was about twenty years older.

They walked inside the mission and Jordan flicked on the lights. They had entered a large open room about the size of a gymnasium. Fluorescent lights buzzed overhead. A couple of small offices were walled off near the front door, and the center of the room contained long rows of tables, piled high with food and supplies. "Would you like some refreshment? Jordan asked. Before they could answer, the French girl appeared with a two-liter bottle of lemonade and filled glass cups for the guests. Lydia and her dad each took one.

Jordan led them into one of the offices, which also contained a lot of boxes—these were filled with cans of mushroom soup—and they sat on wooden chairs around a paper-littered desk. "So, how may I help you?" Jordan said.

"Oh, no agenda here," Frank said. "I just want to hear more about what you do. I'm chatting with different folks who are working in the Holy Land. Like I said on the phone, I'm with Global Relief and Outreach, and we're debating whether to start up a ministry here."

"This town could always use more development workers," Jordan said. "Here at the Lighthouse, we provide only a little food for Palestinians living in the West Bank. It is difficult for us to find jobs, and many of our families are hungry. The people here need so much more than we can offer. They need shelter when their homes are destroyed by bombs, they need counseling when their fathers and brothers are killed, they need furniture and household supplies and just about anything else you can think of." His words rushed out of him like water out of a fire hose. "And that is just for crisis relief. What our people really need are advocates, those who will fight for justice on behalf of Palestinians—"

The French girl with dreadlocks poked her head into the office and leaned against the doorpost. "Lydia, you are bored, no? Come, I will take you from here. I will show you around this place." Lydia liked the way all of the girl's words seemed to have the wrong vowels. She said *thees* for *this* and *frohm* for *from.*

Lydia stood up right away, then remembered to look at her dad for permission. He nodded, and Lydia followed the girl toward the back of the building.

"I am Claire," the girl said. "I am from France, but I've been living here in Bethlehem for these four years. I left my home to get away from my Christian parents. Ooh, but they were harsh! Now I work here in this Christian ministry. How do you like that?"

Lydia admired how Claire laughed at herself.

Back in the warehouse, the four other young people were standing at one of the rows of tables. It was covered with all sorts of breads, and the gang was sorting it into piles. They waved a greeting to Lydia and kept working, laughing all the while. Another row of tables contained canned foods, and still another had sacks of rice, flour, and beans. On the far walls were several doors leading to outside. In front of the doors was a counter separating the warehouse area from a small waiting area where people came to get food.

But what caught Lydia's eye was the wall-to-wall portraits of Palestinian men, women, teenagers, and children. Some people were laughing as if at some outrageous joke. Some looked haunting in their sorrow. Some were caught in the middle of an action—like hugging or dancing or running. All the faces were fascinating, each telling a different story.

"Who are all these people?" Lydia asked.

Claire laughed. "I like to make photographs. Jordan asked me to take photos of the people we help. That way, we remember why we do this work."

"Whoa." Lydia didn't know what else to say. She just kept moving from one picture to another. The impact of the portrait gallery was powerful.

"Come," Claire said after a moment, "let us go help the boys."

The "boys" were still sorting bread—dumping the moldy stuff and separating the sliced bread from the specialty loaves. Claire and Lydia moved in beside them. When Frank and Jordan joined them a half-hour later, Lydia had been named the fastest-learning recruit ever.

"That is good," Jordan said half-seriously. "We need here someone who can work. These items must be sorted by six tomorrow morning, and you jokers have barely started." Jordan turned to Frank. "We collect leftover food from grocery stores and restaurants each evening and spend much of the night sorting it."

"We?" someone said with a friendly snort, tossing a hard dinner roll at their fearless leader.

Jordan smiled. He picked up the roll and threw it into the trash bin. "Back to work," he said good-naturedly. "Last time we tossed food, we did not sleep until daylight."

"We?" the guy said again, this time tossing a bagel with a bite out of it at Jordan.

"Well," Jordan said, catching the bagel and throwing it into the trash in one smooth motion, "someone must be here in the morning to do the important work." Jordan winked at Lydia.

"The fun part, you mean," the snorter said, laughing now. "You get to give away the food."

"You should see this place in morning," Jordan said to Frank. "It is wild scene. We have maybe five volunteers to give food on three mornings every week, from six to ten. But I need maybe twenty to make this machine run smoothly."

"What are the requirements for getting food?" Frank asked.

Jordan shrugged. "We give food to anyone who comes."

"Really? They don't need to fill out an application or anything like that? Don't you have some people taking advantage of the system—people who don't really need the help?"

"We just want to give food," Jordan said. "We do not like for food to be wasted. Besides, if people are willing to come here and face the madness, they are desperate."

Everyone laughed.

"It is not so bad," Claire said. "It is true that many people come here each day, but Jordan's system runs them through quite quickly."

"Yeah," the American guy said, "and they do have to show ID and give some info about themselves before they get food. We track it with a state-of-the-art computer program."

"Plus there are benches and playground equipment out there to keep the waiting people happy," someone else added.

"Come," Jordan said. "You are ruining my image. I almost had him believing I could do this thing with one eye closed."

"I'm very impressed!" Frank said—and Lydia could see he really was. When they had gone to the Olivers', Frank had kept his "nice" face on. Now he looked like a kid who had just found a new memory card for his PSP.

"Don't forget that Claire goes around taking pictures and talking with folks as they wait," another person said. "She's got a gift."

"Yes," Jordan said. "Truly, she does."

Claire smiled a little as they talked about her, and kept sorting bread.

"Is that when you share the gospel?" Frank asked.

Claire looked up sharply.

The American kid shook his head. "Nah, man," he said. "We don't shove Christianity down their throats."

"Just bread," someone said.

"Who is to say that we have all the right answers?" Claire asked.

The others nodded or shrugged in agreement. Lydia could hardly believe it. They were doing Christian ministry without even necessarily believing that Christianity was the truth the world needed.

Frank chuckled. "Ah," he said. "Humble, too." Lydia waited. He would say something else. She knew he would. He did: "May I never boast except in the cross of our Lord Jesus Christ, through which the world has been crucified to me, and I to the world."

Lydia knew that was in the Bible somewhere, but she couldn't remember the chapter and verse. Frank spoke the words very quietly, but everyone looked up from their sorting for a moment.

"We do not quote the Bible, also," Jordan said—and everyone turned back to their work. "It offends too many people. We come in love."

Frank nodded, but his face looked now looked like the battery on his PSP had died.

"They have so much potential!" Frank said as he and Lydia walked home. "They're doing exactly the right thing. If only they would take it a step further and give them the Bread of Life as well. They offer people so much help . . . why don't they offer them Jesus?"

Lydia let him rant on. She didn't know what to think. She certainly liked the Lighthouse gang *way* more than the Olivers. But it made her feel weird inside to think that they might not even believe in Jesus.

10

Suspected

As soon as they got back to the Nativity Hotel, Lydia went to the computer. She didn't know what she was hoping for more—a message from Ben or one from Marcus. She got both. Plus both were online. As a bonus, her best friend, Amy, was logged on too.

Life was good!

thelid1: hi ben
grtbenmn: lyd!
grtbenmn: quick
grtbenmn: shes coming
grtbenmn: r u there?
thelid1: who
grtbenmn: hink

"Hink" was their nickname for Ben's tutor, Gretchen Hinkle, a retired schoolteacher who now volunteered to work for Global Relief and Outreach in Liberia. Frank had originally hired her to tutor Lydia, and the older lady had turned out to have an outrageous sense of humor—but was she ever strict!

grtbenmn: shes up to something
grtbenmn: i need ur help figuring it out
grtbenmn: somethings weird

thelid1: tell me more

thelid1: ben! where r u

"grtbenmn" is away from his computer at 8:22:53 PM.

Marcusicool: hi lydia

thelid1: hi marcus

Marcusicool: wassup

thelid1: not much

thelid1: went to galilee today

Marcusicool: kewl

thelid1: how did u get online?

thelid1: I thot ur dad disconnected u

Marcusicool: i got my ways

Marcusicool: ;)

Marcusicool: u should come over again

thelid1: i wish

thelid1: i got in trouble 4 that

Marcusicool: u did?

Marcusicool: ur friend sarah didn't tell me that

thelid1: u talked to sarah?

Marcusicool: yeah, I saw her

Marcusicool: oh, where r u gonna b tomorrow?

thelid1: a palestinian church

thelid1: here in Bethlehem

thelid1: how bout u?

Marcusicool: ur in bethlehem?

Marcusicool: whoa!

Marcusicool: oh my loser sister says hi

thelid1: tell her hi

Marcusicool: u shouldnt hang with her, tho

Marcusicool: she acts sweet, but shes up to no good

Redhead2831: lydia! my darling!

thelid1 (to amy): my sweet amy! i miss you!!!!!!!

Redhead2831: how r u????!!!!!!!

Redhead2831: i miss u 2 !!! xoxo

Redhead2831: u **HAVE** to come home

thelid1 (intended for ben): tell me more

thelid1: whoops! sry

thelid1: whats going on in Indy???

Redhead2831: who r u talking 2

Redhead2831: im in the church play again

Redhead2831: and i cant do it w/o u!!!!

Redhead2831: *come home!!!!!*

Redhead2831: soooo . . . .

thelid1: kooool!!! what part r u playing!

thelid1: I want 2 b there!!!

Redhead2831: who

Redhead2831: r

Redhead2831: u

Redhead2831: talking

Redhead2831: 2

Redhead2831: ???????

Redhead2831: J J J J

thelid1: J

thelid1: someone very cute!!! J J

Besides trying to chat with these three VIPs at once, Lydia was trying to ignore a V*un*IP in the chair beside her. He was a kid about her age, and he'd shown up at the computers about the same time she had. He had zits all over his face and wore geeky clothes. He plunked down beside Lydia and started blaring music from the one of the other computers—Lydia *hated* reggae—and he kept glancing over at her.

"Would you like gum?" the kid asked about the same time Ben logged off. He had an accent that sounded a little like Muhammed's, but some of his words sounded almost American. He offered a friendly smile.

"Uh, sure," Lydia said. She didn't want to be rude.

"I'm Mitri," he said as she unwrapped the gum.

"Uh, I'm Lydia."

"Nice to meet you."

"Yeah, you too." She chewed the gum, but made sure not to catch his eye again as she went back to IM-ing.

Her dad walked up behind her and said her name in a strangely formal tone of voice. Lydia could easily ignore Mitri, but she could ignore the VmostIP, her dad, only long enough to type "brb" to Marcus.

"Yeah, Dad?"

"Could I talk to you a minute?" His voice still sounded a bit odd, as if he were about to deliver some bad news."

"Uh. Sure. Hold on."

She quickly wrote "g2g" to both Marcus and Amy (since Ben was already gone), logged out, and swung around in her chair.

Frank looked like he was about to say something, but then changed his mind. He turned to Mitri, but then ended up saying nothing to him too. He finally spoke to Lydia. "Why don't you come up to the room a minute."

It wasn't a question.

As soon as they got to their suite, Frank shut the door and turned to Lydia. She sat on the chair by the desk. "I've got to ask you a question, Lydia," he said in voice that sounded as though he couldn't believe what was happening.

"Is something wrong?" Lydia asked.

Frank sat down. "How much money do you have here?"

79

Lydia remembered that she had left the money she won from Sarah on her dresser. Whoops! "Umm . . . about a hundred shekels. I think."

Frank didn't say anything for a moment, and Lydia squirmed.

"That's a lot of money," he finally said. "Where did you get it?"

Lydia had promised Sarah she wouldn't rat her out. Why did she ever take that stupid bet? She looked down at the floor and squirmed. "Sarah gave it to me," she said, then added, "It only adds up to like twenty-five bucks."

"That's a lot of money to give away."

"Yeah. That's what I told her. Should I give it back to her?"

"I think that would be a good idea."

"Okay."

Lydia started to turn toward the door so she could get back to the computer, glad the problem could be resolved so easily.

"Wait, Lydia," Frank said, still leaning up against the door. "You didn't get that money from the Olivers, did you?"

This time Lydia stared at him. *"What?"*

Frank didn't look away. "Did you, Lydia?"

"No, Dad!" she said. "Of course not!" Then she turned her back on him, walked calmly to her room, and shut the door.

She would never—*not ever!*—talk to that man again.

"I love you, Daddy!" Lydia nearly screamed. She didn't care that Mitri must have thought she was a total moron.

It was the next morning and they were down in the computer room again. Lydia had gotten up early and slipped past her sleeping dad, still furious that he had questioned her about taking money from the Olivers. She was determined to ignore him all day. She had come to the computer room first thing, but no one was online. She had been writing a blog entry when Mitri showed up. He really wasn't all that bad. And then Frank had come down to surprise her with this. A new cell phone!

So much for ignoring her dad.

"Shhh!" Frank whispered, pulling her into a hug, laughing. "I know you do. I love you, too."

She stared adoringly at her new phone, a sleek, blue Razr that came with Internet access and free music downloads. "I can really call home whenever I want?"

"You bet. You can even check your e-mail with it."

Lydia screamed with delight and held the phone out for Mitri to see. He smiled as if she were showing him a dinosaur egg. Lydia gave him points for at least trying to be interested.

"Your mother would have said I'm spoiling you—" Frank began.

"No! No! You're not!" Not that Lydia really knew what her mother would think. Nadia Barnes had died in a plane crash when Lydia was six. But from what Lydia had heard, her mother had been the life of the party. She probably would have bought a phone for Lydia long ago.

"—but," Frank said loudly, indicating with his eyes that she was interrupting, "I'm giving it to you for your safety. I want you to have it fully charged whenever you step away from me and to have the ringer on loud so you'll always be able to hear me calling."

"I promise!"

"Remember, this phone is for your safety. The fun stuff is secondary. I paid for a service that you should be able to use in any country. And I put myself on speed dial. Just hit the number 1 and it'll call me."

Lydia was examining the phone from all angles. "It's a camera phone!" she squealed.

"Nice!" Mitri said.

Frank smiled. "Yes, and it takes short videos. One of these days I'll try to help you figure out how to use that for your blog. I'm still trying to figure out how to put pictures on mine."

"Umm . . . I already know how." Lydia looked at Mitri, and they both laughed. Her dad may've known everything about world travel and been the best downhill skier in the universe, but he was totally clueless when it came to computers.

"You do?" Frank said.

Lydia laughed. "Daddy! Tell me you're joking! You *have* to know how to add pics and vids to your blog." She whipped open her phone and logged on to the Internet. In a moment, she was at her site—www.LydiaBarnes.com. From there, she went to her blog.

"Nice!" Mitri said. "Please give me the address so I can look at it here." He opened up her site on his computer, and Frank moved in to look over her shoulder.

"Wow!" Frank said. "Look! You've got so many comments!"

She laughed again. She was too happy to roll her eyes at him. "Of course. That's what blogging is all about—staying connected with my peeps."

"Peeps?"

"My people, dad. My friends!"

"Oh." He shook his head and picked up his jacket. "Well, let's quit exploring the World Wide Web and start exploring the wide, wide world."

Frank had given Lydia a pretty blue cell phone carrier to hang on her hip, but that was so out of style. She put the phone in her little purse along with the one hundred shekels. She'd have to remember to give Sarah her money back as soon as she could. Ten minutes later, they were hailing a cab outside the hotel.

"Oh, by the way," Frank said a little too casually when they were settled in the back seat, "I'm sorry for making you feel bad last night. You told me you got the money from Sarah, so you must have gotten it from Sarah."

Lydia nodded slightly. He didn't sound convincing, and she didn't want to talk about it.

"Why did she give you so much money, though? I'm just curious."

Lydia wanted to tell him about the bet, but she couldn't betray her friend. She shrugged and looked out the window. "She insisted."

"Okay," Frank said. He didn't mention the money again all day.

But Lydia knew he didn't believe her.

11
Near Disaster

The Old City in Jerusalem was bizarre. And busy. And fun. And spiritual.

They entered through the Dung Gate again, the place where people used to get rid of the sewage from everyone in Jerusalem.

"Man alive!" her dad said. "It must have stunk back then! I'm glad I live in the time of modern plumbing."

"Sure you are," Lydia said. "That's why you have latrine-building contests whenever you go backpacking with Uncle Joe."

They walked through the Jewish Quarter, passing by the Shalom Guesthouse where Sarah and her parents lived and arriving at the Western Wall. To get into the Wall area, they had to pass through a security checkpoint with armed guards and metal detectors, just like at the airport. Once inside, they were in a large, open courtyard with people from all over the world milling around, talking, and praying. The Wall itself was about four stories high and made of huge, rectangular, yellowish stones. There was a small, wooden wall that separated the area into two parts, one side for men and the other for women. Most of the others praying were Jewish people dressed in traditional clothes. The men wore black suits with a white shirt and no tie, and they wore big black hats.

Lydia went on the women's side, Frank on the men's, and went up to the wall to pray silently. Up close, the Wall was all craggy, with lots of cracks and crevices. Little pieces of paper were stuck in some of the cracks. Lydia knew they were prayer requests people had left there. She started to reach for one so she could see what it said, but then she pulled her hand away. When she started to think about how this wall had been part of the Temple where God had once made his home, she wanted to behave with great respect. This God deserved her awe.

She finished praying and walked backward out of the prayer area, just like most of the others were doing. It was as if no one wanted to disrespect God by turning their backs on him. Frank was waiting for her outside the women's section.

They walked along the Cardo, an ancient street that had been built by the Romans, about the size of an eight-lane highway. The stones beneath their feet formed an interesting crisscross pattern and were worn smooth. Lydia loved the old Roman pillars and could imagine the buzz of life that must have taken place there once upon a time.

Soon they entered the Muslim Quarter, the part of the Old City where Muslims lived. The streets here were narrow and lined with tiny shops selling everything from trinkets to computers. Every space seemed crowded with people—haggling over prices in the shops, buying vegetables from food carts, or just walking along the narrow streets.

"Next time we're here, we'll walk the Via Dolorosa and visit the Church of the Holy Sepulcher," Frank said. He sounded as excited as a kid talking about the gifts he expected for Christmas, which was just a few days away. Today was Thursday and Christmas was next Monday.

"The holy what?" Lydia asked.

"It's the place where they say Jesus was crucified and buried," Frank said. "But now it's time to get back to the hotel."

Getting back was not as simple as they'd expected.

After walking back to the Dung Gate, Frank hailed a cab for the ride to Bethlehem. As they pulled up to the security checkpoint outside Bethlehem, they saw a mob of people surrounding another car that was stopped by the guard station. The driver quickly pulled over to the side of the road. "We'd better get out of here," Frank said. Something horribly wrong was going on, and Lydia was glad her dad was trying to get out of the action rather than into it—for once.

But it was too late.

A guard waved them over. "What's your business here?" he said gruffly.

"We're heading to our hotel in Bethlehem," Frank said as calmly as he could. Lydia noticed he was chewing on his bottom lip, which was a sure sign he was nervous. The cab driver was speaking rapidly in either Hebrew or Arabic, Lydia didn't know which.

The guard took their passports and disappeared in the direction of the checkpoint. A moment later, the mob turned away from the other car and headed toward their cab. The cab driver was shouting and waving his arms, then he leaped out of the cab and ran away. Then the guard who had taken their passports ran straight into the crowd and starting pushing people aside. Suddenly a gunshot boomed out, and people scattered—to reveal a dead man lying on the ground.

Lydia didn't know whether to follow the cab driver or stay in the car with her dad. She clung to Frank's arm, trying not to scream in terror. "Dad, we need to get out of here," she pleaded.

But Frank now seemed determined to stick around. "I want to find out what's going on," he said. Then he kissed her forehead. "It'll be okay, Peachoo." Lydia wasn't so sure. "Besides, that guy still has our passports." They got out of the car and walked toward the soldier who had been trying to shove people away from the car.

It appeared that an Israeli soldier shot a Palestinian man who was standing near the checkpoint, and then a bunch of others mobbed the soldier. But every person who told the story said it a little differently. Some said that the Palestinian man had attacked the soldier. Others said the man was just walking by when he was shot for no reason. Who knew the real story?

Frank and Lydia were finally allowed to leave, and they walked about a mile back to the Nativity Hotel. Lydia went straight to the computer. Her hands had finally quit shaking, and she *had* to tell Ben about what happened. He wasn't online, but there was an e-mail in her inbox from him. He was yelling at her—and yes, YOU CAN YELL ONLINE!—for ignoring him the day before. He had important stuff to tell her.

She wrote back right away to tell him that maybe *she* had important stuff to deal with too. Sheesh. Then she filled him in on the shooting in the little town of Bethlehem. "ill never b able 2 sing that xmas song again without breaking out in a sweat," she wrote.

"just b glad it wasnt you" That was Ben's entire message when Lydia opened her e-mail the next morning.

Lydia heaved a big sigh and then saw Mitri walking toward her. She smiled at him, not even noticing his zits anymore. He had very nice eyes. He wasn't as cute as Marcus, of course, but he was very nice. "You have a phone call," Mitri said. "Over there." He gestured toward the lobby.

Surprised, Lydia went to the house phone near the front desk.

"Lydia! Are you okay?"

It was Marcus. Marcus!

"Yeah. I'm okay. Why? And how did you get this number?" The hotel manager was staring at her beneath his bushy eyebrows, and Lydia knew she'd have to make this quick.

"Brenda told me. You know that Canadian girl from the Olivers' guesthouse? I keep bumping into her everywhere. She seems to be keeping track of you."

"Oh." Lydia still didn't know why he was calling. And she sure didn't know why Brenda was spying on her.

"Anyway, I can't believe that guy got killed right in front of you!"

"Yeah, it was terrible." Lydia shivered at the memory. The manager was hovering. "Hey," Lydia said, "I've got a cell phone now. Call me on that." She got a bit flustered trying to figure out her number, especially when she saw Mitri watching her, but she finally found it. Then she ran to her hotel room and shut the door to get some privacy.

"Umm, I won't be able to talk long," Marcus said when he called back. "I'm supposed to be making one quick call," he said. "You know that whole 'disconnected' kick my dad's on."

"That's okay. How did you find out about the shooting?"

"We saw you on TV," Marcus said.

"I was on TV?"

"Yeah. When your dad was talking to the police or whatever, the camera panned over to you."

Lydia wanted to hear more—yikes! how had she looked?—but then she heard Marcus whisper, "Get lost!" and a small scream from a girl. She guessed it was his sister. "Oh, and Michelle says hi."

The rest of the conversation was really just Marcus and Michelle fighting. But Lydia still sang a happy tune when they hung up. There was most definitely something going on between them—and she was downright merry.

Lydia skipped back down to the lobby, where she found Frank chatting with the hotel manager—trying to get some inside information about the town of Bethlehem, apparently. His whole agenda for today was to spend time in the West Bank. Lydia's agenda was to not be bored.

Mitri was still at the computer.

"So, are you visiting here, or what?" she asked. She was in a good mood and Mitri looked to be her most likely companion. She plopped down on a stuffed chair beside him and swung her legs over the arms of the chair.

"Oh, no, my mother works here. I just stay about all the time. It is better than being home alone." He continued clicking his mouse. It looked like he was browsing through Web sites faster than Lydia could talk. Which was saying a lot.

"What about school?" Lydia asked.

"We are on a school holiday right now. Unfortunately."

"You like school?"

"Yes, very much. Recently, my brother graduated from Bethlehem University. I wish to go there someday and become a lawyer."

"Wow."

"Or maybe a Lutheran pastor," he said. He finally logged out of the browser and turned away from the computer to look at her.

Lydia was surprised to hear he was a Christian, but she didn't say anything. "I'm going to be an author," Lydia said. "Either that or the President of the United States." Everyone always laughed when she said that, but she wasn't kidding.

Mitri just nodded as if she had announced she'd brushed her hair that morning. "I know!" he said, clearly having had just come up with a brilliant idea. "Would you like for me to show you around Bethlehem today?"

"You sound like every taxi driver in Jerusalem," Lydia said with a laugh. "I take you to Bethlehem," she said, trying to mimic the cabbies' thick Arabic accent. "Just one hundred fifty shekels." Her pronunciation wasn't perfect, but it was close enough.

Mitri laughed. "For you, one hundred shekels," he said. Then he stood up. "No, this is for fun only. Something to do."

Lydia wanted to go, but it seemed very unlikely. "I don't think my dad would let me." She glanced over at her dad, who was still deep in conversation with the manager.

"Why not?" Mitri looked at him too. "Would he not trust me?"

"He wouldn't trust *me*," she said, swinging her legs from the armrest and leaning back into the cushions.

"Why is that?" he asked, sitting down again beside Lydia. "Did you do something wrong?"

"He *thinks* I did."

"What does he think you did?" He leaned back into the cushions just as she was doing.

Lydia covered her face with her fingers. "He thinks I stole some money."

Mitri turned to look at her seriously. "Did you?"

Lydia hoped her glare showed him how inappropriate that question was. "No!"

Mitri shrugged. "Then why does he think so?"

"Well, I'm not sure he thinks that. But it seems that way." Lydia scooted forward to the edge of the chair and explained the whole story about the money going missing at the Christian Hope Center and how Mrs. Oliver had accused Lydia of stealing it and then how her dad had found the money Sarah had given her.

Mitri sat forward. "Maybe it is time to solve that mystery— just like on *Spy Kids.*"

"What?" Lydia asked. "You've seen *Spy Kids?*"

Mitri sighed. "Lydia, I live in Bethlehem, not on the moon."

"Oh," Lydia said. "Right."

Frank finished his conversation and walked toward Lydia. He winked at her and said he was going up to the room for a minute.

Lydia had to smile. Ben would have loved hanging out with Mitri. "Okay," she said. "Let's solve this mystery. Where do we begin?"

12
Betrayed

ou must go back to the scene of the crime," Mitri said.

"Me?" Lydia said. "Why not you? They don't know you, so you could snoop around without anyone suspecting anything."

"I cannot go to Jerusalem."

"Sure, you can. It's just six miles."

"Lydia," Mitri said quietly, "did you notice that I am Palestinian?" He held up his hands around his face.

Lydia looked at him as if he had just said that Frank was her dad. "Uh, yeah. What's that got to do with the price of gas?"

"Pardon?"

"It's just a saying. What's the big deal about you being Palestinian?"

"Everything," he said. "I cannot leave the West Bank."

"You can't leave?"

"No. You may have noticed the wall around our city. Did you not go through a checkpoint when you came here."

"Yeah, but they took one look at our passports and waved us through."

"Yes, they let *you* through. But they would not let me. I must stay here."

Lydia stared at him for a moment, waiting for the punch line. When it didn't come, she said, "So, you're like a prisoner here?"

"Exactly. I can go wherever I want here in Bethlehem so long as there is no curfew, which there isn't right now—"

"But you can't leave?"

"No."

"But I thought your dad lives in Jerusalem."

"He does."

"So you never see him?"

"I do see him every couple of days when he comes to Bethlehem to visit my mother and me. He has a permit that allows him to travel to the West Bank. But he must go back every night."

"You mean, your mom and dad are still married?"

"Of course!"

Lydia felt horrible. She couldn't imagine living that way. "That's really bad, Mitri. Why is this allowed? Shouldn't the United Nations send in troops or something?"

He looked at her, surprised. "You want to be President of the United States, and you really do not know?"

"Know what?" She hated feeling dumb.

"*Your* government is supporting the Israeli troops that keep us locked up here in our own lands."

Lydia thought briefly of Sarah and how she seemed so afraid of Palestinians. "But what about all the bombings?" she asked.

"Lydia, those are terrible acts of violence committed by a few extremists." Mitri brushed the air with his hand and leaned back in his seat. "It does not matter. You can do nothing about it in anyway."

"Why? 'Cause I'm just a kid?" Lydia asked.

"Exactly."

"Hey! Kids can change the world," Lydia said. She was just getting ready to give a little speech about how she and Ben had talked to one of the top rebel leaders in Liberia and got him to see the world differently, but Mitri stopped her short.

"How can you change the world if you cannot even prove that you are innocent of stealing a little money?"

That was enough to motivate Lydia to solve this mystery for real. "You know what?" she said, reaching into her pocket for her cell phone. "We need to talk to my friend Sarah who lives in Jerusalem. She lives sort of near the Christian Hope Center, and maybe she can help."

Lydia had programmed the number to Shalom Guesthouse into her cell phone, and she dialed it now.

When Sarah got on the line, Lydia said, "Hey, Trouble."

Sarah must have recognized her voice right away because she said, "You're the one in trouble."

"Touché," Lydia said. If only Sarah wasn't so right about that. "Hey, my dad says I have to give you that money back."

"What!" Sarah said, sounding angry. "You told him about the bet?"

"'Course not," Lydia said. But she probably should have. "I promised I wouldn't, and I didn't. But he does know you gave it to me."

There was silence on the other end of the line for a moment—and for the first time Lydia wondered where Sarah had gotten the money. Lydia couldn't believe how stupid she had been. Sarah should be her prime suspect! And here she was trying not to admit that she suspected Marcus! And even Brenda.

Then Sarah broke into her thoughts. "It was nice of you not to tell. Thanks."

The tone of Sarah's voice showed that she really was grateful. Lydia shook herself. Why was she suspecting all her friends? Sarah didn't even know the Olivers. "No problem. Now I just need to find out who really stole that money so my dad will trust me again."

"Are you going to hire a private detective?" Sarah asked.

Lydia glanced at Mitri, who was listening to her every word. She held the phone closer to him so he could hear Sarah's side of the conversation. "That'd be too much money. Besides, he'd need to be able to go into the Christian Hope Center, and then we'd have to get all the adults to approve. No, we need to be our own detectives."

"So what shall we do?"

Lydia smiled. Sarah was onboard. "Well, someone has to go back to the scene of the crime."

"Meaning me?"

Lydia laughed. "Yeah, meaning you. Will you?"

"Of course I will. What should I be looking for?"

"I don't know," Lydia said. She sighed. "Maybe we should interview the Olivers to create a list of suspects." She needed to get people other than her friends on that list. Next she'd be suspecting Mitri.

"Maybe I can just watch the place and see if people are hanging around," Sarah suggested.

"Good idea," Lydia said.

Mitri nodded energetically.

"Or maybe we can interview nearby shop owners to see if they've had any trouble." Sarah's voice lifted. She was getting into this too.

Lydia was impressed. "That's good! This may work." Lydia felt a rush of energy and could hardly wait to begin.

"Oh!" Sarah said suddenly, and Lydia could hear her slam something down. "Ben wanted to chat with us at ten this morning." Lydia glanced at the clock. "That's just two minutes from now."

"What?" Lydia said. "How do you know Ben?"

"Can you get to a computer?" Sarah asked.

"Yeah . . ."

"Good. I'll send you an invitation for a group chat."

Lydia felt like she had just caught her grandma howling at the moon. The information entering her brain was too weird to accept. She walked over to the computer desk and logged in. When the invitation for "Sarah's Room" showed up, she clicked "accept."

Mitri sat down beside her, asking her what was going on. Lydia didn't trust herself to say anything. Or to write anything.

She wanted to demand: how did u get *my* friend's screen name? She was probably chatting with Marcus too. And maybe Amy. This was so unfair! Lydia sat there staring at the blinking cursor until a message popped up saying that grtbenmn had entered the room.

Sarah must have had Ben's message already typed because an instant later she had said hi to "benny-bear" with a pathetic heart-filled smiley face.

Then the weirdest thing of all happened: Ben started flirting with Sarah.

Seriously.

sarhstar: hi benny-bear 😊
grtbenmn: hi sare-bear
grtbenmn: i was just thinking bout
sarhstar: u were?
grtbenmn: yeah, u really helped me last night
grtbenmn: that was nice
sarhstar: good
sarhstar: so, how did it go today?
grtbenmn: it was tough
sarhstar: im sry
grtbenmn: tx
grtbenmn: im actually kind of scared
grtbenmn: dont tell lydia
sarhstar: 😕
sarhstar: ummm . . . say hello to lydia
grtbenmn: oh . . . r u there lid?

Lydia was in a state of shock, but she was there. Still, she couldn't get her fingers to move.

> **grtbenmn:** hi
> **sarhstar:** u should tell her anyway
> **grtbenmn:** r u there lid?
> **grtbenmn:** lid?
> **sarhstar:** shes there
> **sarhstar:** tell her, ben
> **grtbenmn:** lid?

If she had been sweet, Lydia would have forced her fingers the press the letters "h" and "i." Lydia, however, was feeling anything but sweet at this moment. She felt betrayed. By both of them. Not that she had a crush on Ben or that she was the only one who was allowed to be friends with either of them, but something was still wrong with this picture.

> **grtbenmn:** y dont u want to talk?
> **grtbenmn:** r u 2 busy chatting with Marcus?

Lydia barely stopped her fingers from typing a nasty reply. She was surprised at how angry she was at the moment. But she wasn't feeling mean. It was mostly sad. Her second-best friend, Ben, was all chummy with her new friend Sarah, who was more and more making Lydia feel queasy, and to top it all off she was suspected of stealing money, mistrusted by her dad, and freaked out about this place where somebody seemed to get blown up or shot every other day.

Without typing a word, Lydia logged out, shut down the computer, and walked slowly to her room.

She hated her life.

"You hate your life?" Frank asked, looking very confused. "Because your friends are friends?"

Clearly he did not understand girls.

"Dad!" She had enough frustration in her voice to make flowers wilt.

But her dad just shrugged. "So, how are you and Mitri getting along?"

With a deep sigh, Lydia gave up on throwing a pity party for herself. No one seemed to be showing up for it anyway. "He seems cool," she said. "He wanted to take me around Bethlehem today."

"Did you say yes?"

Lydia looked at her dad to see if he was just messing with her. "I didn't think you'd let me."

"Well, I got a good report about him from his mother's boss," Frank said with a little grin.

Wait—her dad was checking out her friends behind her back?

"Later this afternoon we'll head back to Jerusalem," he said, "but I don't mind if you hang out with Mitri this morning. I have to meet with a Christian pastor in a few minutes here, and it might be boring for you."

"Cool!" Lydia suddenly realized that she'd walked away from Mitri without even saying good-bye. "Thanks, Daddy," she said, and tore down the stairs to find him.

13

Brokenhearted

Frank went off to his meeting right after lunch, and Lydia was running free.

Mitri led her down the cobblestone streets toward the edge of Bethlehem. It was cloudier today than it had been before, and it felt much chillier. If only it would snow for Christmas! The stone buildings created cool pockets of shadow that Lydia tried to avoid as they walked together down the narrow street.

She was surprised at how safe she felt in the West Bank. A few people looked at her, clearly noticing she was a stranger, but they usually smiled when she looked back. Most people didn't pay her much attention. Grownups seemed busy getting to wherever they were going and boys walked around with arms around each other, off on their own adventures. Maybe they weren't all terrorists after all.

Mitri took Lydia out of the city to a field where shepherds were keeping their sheep. Just like in the Bible story. The field looked like an open space in Colorado, hilly and rocky with very few trees. Her dad had taken her to Colorado Springs a couple years ago, and they had driven through a no-man's land where only yucca plants and cactuses could grow. It looked about the same here, except that there were bearded men wearing cloth head coverings sat on the rocks and watched a bunch of scraggly-looking sheep.

When they came to a little cave in the side of a hill, Mitri told Lydia to go inside.

"No way!" she said. She could smell it even from outside.

"Come," he said, stepping in front of her to lead the way.

Lydia followed. She could see the remains of a campfire on the sandy floor in the middle, and bunches of wool stuck to the rocks. The place smelled like a barn.

"Shepherds keep their sheep here during a storm or when it is too cold to be outside," Mitri said.

"Kind of like a stable?"

"Yes. And there is the manger." He pointed to a pile of hay shoved in the darkest corner of the cave.

"Ugh," Lydia said. She tried to imagine Baby Jesus lying in that pile of old grass but couldn't pull it off. Wouldn't there be bugs all over him? Ick. "I wouldn't want to hang out here long."

"It is not bad once you get used to it," Mitri said. "But now let me show you something amazing."

They walked back into town, and rain started to fall on the cobblestone streets.

Lydia ducked under the awning in front of a little shop. "I thought it was supposed to be a desert here."

"No, it rains here often, and it even snows in the winter." He walked on, not picking up his speed at all. "A little rain won't hurt you. We are going to the Jacir Palace Hotel now. It is the pride of our town." As they walked, he pretended he was her tour guide and showed his sense of humor about all of the tourist traps in the Holy Land. He said, "Here is the carwash where Jesus worked as a teenager. And over there is the Internet café where the disciples used to hang out."

Lydia almost felt guilty for laughing so hard. If Ben could see her right now, he'd probably be just as miffed as she'd been about him IMing Sarah. But Mitri was just so funny.

He led her down a main street toward a towering, white stone building with beautiful arches and pillars adorning its front. Her brain told her it was just a hotel, but her heart knew it truly was a palace.

Mitri guided her around the building to show her the beautiful pools and gorgeous flower gardens. Once inside, Lydia realized the building was even more vast than it appeared from the outside. They discovered new ballrooms restaurants around each corner.

"Your former President Jimmy Carter stayed here once," he said. "But very few other dignitaries are willing to come to the occupied lands. Most of them stay in Jerusalem."

"When I'm President," Lydia said, "I'll stay here. For sure."

After an hour of exploring the Palace, Mitri said it was time to get going.

"But we haven't seen everything yet," Lydia said.

"Your father made me promise to get you home by 1:30 so you can go to Jerusalem." He began walking toward the front lobby.

"I wish you could come with us." Lydia said, falling in step beside him.

"Someday," Mitri said. "My dad is going to apply for permission so I can visit the city. They are more generous with giving permission to Christians than to Muslims, so there is hope."

"Once you apply for permission, how long does it take to get approved?"

"Who knows? Sometimes weeks, sometimes months, sometimes days."

"Mitri," Lydia said, grabbing his arm, "you have to come with us to Jerusalem on Christmas!"

"It's Friday today," Mitri said. "Christmas is Monday. I won't get approved by then." He smiled bravely. "But perhaps I can solve the mystery while you are away."

"So why is it called the Place of the Skull?" Lydia asked her dad in a quiet voice. They were walking toward the Church of the Holy Sepulcher, the church built on the spot where Jesus was said to have been crucified.

The rain had stopped, and they walked slowly along the Via Dolorosa, the path Jesus had likely walked as He carried the cross to his death. They stopped at each "station," where some significant detail was remembered—like where Simon of Cyrene had picked up the cross.

The street—if that was what it could be called, since it was too narrow for any vehicles and even had steps in some places—was lined with tall, narrow stone buildings. Most were shops, and Lydia was amazed at how different they all were. Some were brightly lit stores that reminded her of the mall back home. Others were grungy little spaces lined with Persian rugs, pottery, or souvenirs. The street was crowded with tourists, and merchants constantly hawked their wares, calling out things like, "You buy postcards. Just one American dollar," or "You need olive wood cross. Good souvenir!"

"No one knows for sure if the church is in the actual place where Jesus was crucified," Frank said, his voice hushed. "It was called Golgotha—the Place of the Skull—because the hillside used to be shaped like a skull. We can't see that now because this city is built on top of the ruins of the old city."

"So, do *you* think it's where Jesus was crucified?" Lydia asked.

"Could be," her dad said with a grin. "I leave it as a question."

Just then a small group of Americans—two men and a woman—walked by them, softly singing, "Were you there when they crucified my Lord?" People paid them little attention, and

Lydia figured that was a common way for Christians to worship here in the Holy City.

It made sense. There was something very spiritual about walking in the actual steps of Jesus. She felt as if she were in a mystery movie or something because her neck and head got all tingly.

Frank looked down respectfully while the singers passed, but then went right back to the conversation. "I guess it's kind of like Christmas," he said. "We don't know the exact date of Jesus' birth, but we don't let that stop us from celebrating."

Lydia hardly felt like celebrating. And even though it was December, she couldn't help thinking about Easter. Actually, the whole idea of Easter seemed weird. She'd heard stories about the crucifixion and resurrection all her life, but each step closer to the place of Jesus' death made it so much more real. Too real.

"It's Friday today," she said quietly.

Frank nodded. "Christmas is next week, but for us it's Good Friday, isn't it?"

Good Friday: the day Jesus died.

They turned a corner, and Lydia found herself in a stone courtyard about two the size of a small parking lot. At the far end was a towering white stone church. Well, it was more brown than white since the stone had gotten dirty over the years. From where she was standing, it didn't look much like a church. It looked more like a prison to Lydia, with sturdy stone walls and windows covered in bars. People were entering and exiting through a dark archway in the back left corner of the courtyard. Lydia and her dad stood for a few minutes in the courtyard listening to a tour guide describe the place as the most holy site in the world for Christians—the place that represents where Jesus was crucified, buried, and resurrected.

Once inside, Lydia climbed a narrow stone stairway to pray at the place where they say Jesus died. Moments later, she knelt to touch the flat, rectangular stone where they say his body was prepared for burial.

"Are you ready, Peachoo?" Frank's words startled Lydia. She looked up to see her dad standing beside her, smiling. How long had she been kneeling there, lost in thought? She stood and turned toward the door. They exited the church without speaking another word.

Frank and Lydia walked slowly back through the Old City. Frank led the way toward the Church of the Redeemer, which was supposed to be their next stop. But Lydia was too caught up in the emotions of Easter to do any more touring.

All she could think about was how horrible it must have been for the people who loved Jesus to watch him walk to his death— not only because they loved him so much, but because He was their only hope.

"You go ahead to the next church, Dad," she said. "I'll go back to Sarah's guesthouse and wait for you there. I have to give Sarah her money back anyway." That was the wrong thing to say because it made her remember that her dad still thought she had stolen the money. Would he let her go off by herself now?

"Umm, okay," Frank said after just a brief hesitation. "But be good."

Of course she would, and she hated it that he thought he needed to tell her that. He used to always say, "Have fun!" when they parted company.

Lydia marched on through the narrow, crowded streets of the Old City by herself. Everywhere she looked there were people. There in the Muslim Quarter, she saw dark-haired teenagers wearing American-style clothes laughing and talking ask they walked. There were women carrying babies, kids playing a pickup game of soccer, and the ever-present souvenir hawkers. Most of them were Palestinians who had permission to live in Jerusalem. *Weird,* she thought, *how come Sarah is so afraid of these people?*

Lydia had no fear of getting lost. She had a tourist map, and she had spend hours poring over it at the hotel. Now she enjoyed seeing how the map came to life as she walked on the streets whose names she had memorized. It was like the difference between studying the cheat codes for your favorite gaming system online and actually playing the game with a bunch of friends. Knowing things in your head is not nearly as cool as experiencing them.

As Lydia strolled into the Jewish Quarter, she found herself thinking less about the sights and sounds of the city and more about Jesus. He had known the whole plan from the beginning. Before he came to earth, he had studied the map—he knew exactly what would happen to him. He knew that he would be born as a baby—maybe in that same dingy cave that the shepherds used as a barn—and he knew that he would have to die, even though he was completely innocent. And he still chose to come to earth.

"I would never put up with that!" A Jewish woman wearing a long black coat gave her a funny look and Lydia realized she was talking out loud. She smiled weakly, and the woman crossed the street shaking her head.

Lydia knew in her head that Jesus had to die to pay for her sins, but she didn't get it. Not really. Being falsely accused of stealing money was just about killing her. What if the whole city turned against her? What if *everyone* thought she were guilty of something she hadn't done?

That reminded her, she might as well use this time to go to the Christian Hope Center and interview Mr. and Mrs. Oliver.

Sarah was planning to do some snooping around there, but since Lydia was so close already, she decided it wouldn't hurt to go a few blocks off her route.

As Lydia neared the Christian Quarter of the city, the Jewish crowd thinned and the Palestinian crowd increased. It still surprised her that so many Arabs were Christian.

She walked out the Damascus Gate, which was narrower but much prettier than the Dung Gate—with a cobblestone path and lovely arch—and soon saw the Olivers' guesthouse. Like most of the other buildings, it was made of old white stone, only this one was shorter than most, just two stories. Men were working on it, and Lydia stopped to watch for a few minutes. The wall that had been damaged by the bomb was being rebuilt, and it didn't look much different from the rest of the building.

But of course this was the Olivers' guesthouse, and they wouldn't be here now. They'd be at the bookstore in the Christian Hope Center, a few couple blocks away. Lydia was debating whether to go there when she caught of glimpse of Brenda hurrying toward the Damascus Gate.

"Brenda!" she called.

The blonde head turned her way for an instant, and then hurried on. Lydia was sure Brenda had seen her. Did she still think Lydia had stolen that money and now was avoiding her?

"Fine," she said to herself, and turned back toward the guesthouse. Just then she noticed movement in one of the windows. She took a step forward to see better what it was, and was startled to see eyes peering at her between the shutters—and then quickly disappear.

Lydia suddenly felt very alone. She put her hand in her purse and touched her cell phone. Should she call for help?

Never mind going to the Christian Hope Center. This was getting too creepy. She turned around and walked quickly back toward Sarah's place.

But she didn't get far. Her heart was pounding so loud that she wasn't aware someone was chasing her until she felt a strong hand on her shoulder.

14
Accused

Dad!" Lydia shouted. "Don't do that to me!"

"I didn't mean to startle you," he said. "What are you doing over here? I thought you were headed back to the Shalom Guesthouse."

"I was going to, but then—"

His cell phone rang. "Hold on. Hello? Yes, hi, Katherine." He listened and then looked at Lydia. "Yes, she's right here with me." His face took on a look of concern and he walked in little circles. "We'll be right there." He hung up the phone and began striding in the other direction, toward the Christian Hope Center. "Come on."

"What, Dad?" Lydia asked as she scurried after him.

"That was Mrs. Oliver. The center has been vandalized." He studied her face as he walked. "They think you did it."

"Me?"

"I know. It's crazy." His head sank a little toward his chest and he looked suddenly old to Lydia.

Lydia groaned. "I don't want to go," she said—and even she could hear the desperation in her voice. "Can I meet you at Sarah's?"

"Come on," he said again without slowing his pace.

The letters painted in bright red on the outside wall of the center were sloppy and uneven, as if the "artist" was new to using spray paint. The words were clear, though: "u deserve what u got!"

Lydia shuddered. She didn't like the Olivers much, but she knew they didn't deserve this—or the kind of terror they had experienced the other night.

Mr. and Mrs. Oliver stood with them in front of the Christian Hope Center. Mrs. Oliver's arms kept flying up in the air, looking like windshield wipers pulled up by freak gusts of wind. Mr. Oliver seemed completely calm. Some pedestrians stopped to look at the graffiti.

Frank touched the wall. "The paint's still wet."

"Yes," Mrs. Oliver said with tight lips. "The culprit must have done this just a few minutes ago. It wasn't here when we arrived this morning."

Frank looked at Lydia for just an instant—just enough for her to realize he knew she had been near the place within the last few minutes and had been caught running in the opposite direction. Heat rushed to her face and crept into her neck and shoulders. It wasn't warm outside, but she was sweating.

"Lydia," Mrs. Oliver said in a voice with undisguised accusation, "I have it from a reliable source that you were standing outside our guesthouse not long ago. What were you doing?"

Lydia's sweaty skin grew cold. "I was just looking."

"You may not realize this," Mrs. Oliver said, stepping closer to Lydia and looking in her eyes, "but what happened at the guesthouse with that bomb was an act of the Enemy. We are servants of the Most High God, and those who oppose us will feel the wrath of—"

Frank stepped between Mrs. Oliver and Lydia, and Mrs. Oliver jerked up straight. He placed his arm around his daughter. "Katherine," he said with a hint of warning in his voice, "Lydia herself was traumatized by that event. We are *all* horrified by what happened." He looked down at Lydia, and she could see his eyes pleading with her. "Aren't we, Lydia?"

Lydia nodded. She really was horrified by all that had happened. But she also knew that Mrs. Oliver was hateful and arrogant. And weren't those the kind of people Jesus spoke against the most harshly?

"Wait here," Mrs. Oliver said abruptly. "I'm calling the police."

Lydia grabbed her dad's arm. "I didn't do it, Dad!" she whispered anxiously. "Can we just leave?"

Her dad hesitated. "No. We need to face this. If we run away we'll look guilty. Let's go wait inside."

Lydia grumbled but followed her dad.

As they passed the defaced wall and headed toward the front door, sunlight reflected off something shiny in the bushes and caught her eye. She took a step closer.

It was a can of spray paint.

She reached over to pick it up—and immediately regretted it. They already thought she was guilty, and now she had put her fingerprints all over it. She couldn't just leave it out here. She dropped the can into her purse and followed her dad into the bookstore.

"So sorry to take up your time, Mr. Barnes, Ms. Barnes," the police officer said after a half hour of polite questioning. He was a tall Jewish man wearing jeans and a button-down shirt with a white T-shirt underneath. His ball cap had "New York Giants" on it. He spoke English with hardly any accent at all.

"Glad to help out," Frank said, standing up and putting his sunglasses on. "We want to find this culprit as much as anyone."

Mrs. Oliver sniffed. Lydia doubted anyone wanted to rake someone over the coals as much as Mrs. Oliver did. Thank goodness the policeman hadn't asked to check Lydia's purse. Actually, he didn't seem to take Mrs. Oliver's accusations very seriously. Lydia could hardly blame Mrs. Oliver for suspecting her at first. After all, Lydia had been in the room alone around the time the money was stolen. But now it was all over. Lydia felt like she had just won a spelling bee.

The police officer stood up the same time Lydia did. Mrs. Oliver remained sitting. Lydia hadn't seen adults sulk very often, but she was pretty sure that was what Mrs. Oliver was doing. Mr. Oliver had left the room after five minutes of questioning and Lydia didn't see him anywhere now.

"We do ask you to remain available," the police officer said to Frank. "We may need you for further questioning."

Mrs. Oliver stood up then and looked right at Lydia. "That's right. This isn't over yet, missy. You'll get what you deserve."

As soon as they were out the door, Lydia wanted to complain to her dad about this woman who was making her life so miserable; but she knew Frank Barnes didn't put up with "idle chatter." So Lydia kept her mouth shut.

She glanced at the wall as they walked away from the Christian Hope Center and saw Mr. Oliver scrubbing at the red paint. The brightness had been dulled, but the words were still clear. Lydia suddenly noticed that Mrs. Oliver's parting words were almost exactly the same as what was written on her wall.

Frank walked Lydia to the Shalom Guesthouse, Sarah's parents' place. "I have to go meet with another Christian ministry in town," he said when they arrived. "You stay here with Sarah."

"Okay."

As soon as they were alone in the lobby, Sarah headed for the front door. "Come on, Lydia."

"We should stay here," Lydia said.

Sarah narrowed her eyes. "We have to go to those Christian people who think you stole their money. We have to . . . ehr . . . interview them, remember?"

"I can't go there anymore."

"Fine." Sarah plopped down on a couch. "Why the change?"

Lydia sat down herself, pulling a pillow onto her lap. "Someone vandalized their property, and they think I did it."

"Oh." Sarah looked genuinely sad, and Lydia was glad someone cared. "That's awful."

Lydia bravely shrugged. "My dad won't let me go anywhere alone anymore—for my own protection, he says."

They were quiet for a moment.

"Mrs. Oliver is still convinced it's me, even though the police know it's not."

"Who do the police think it is?" Sarah asked.

Lydia shrugged. "I don't think they care much. They have bigger stuff to deal with. But, like I said, Mrs. Oliver is still trying to pin this on me. We've got to solve this mystery." Suddenly Lydia remembered the paint in her purse. "Oh! I found a can of spray paint in the bushes. Evidence!"

"How will that help?"

Lydia shrugged. "I don't know. I'll write to Ben. He'll have an idea."

Sarah ran to her room to get a notepad to record all their findings, and Lydia went to the computer in the lobby. No one else was in the room. All the tourists were out touring, and even the employees were off cleaning rooms or taking a break.

Ben was online, so Lydia went straight to business.

thelid1: hi ben

grtbenmn: lydia!

grtbenmn: i didnt think u were talking 2 me anymore

thelid1: I nvr said that

grtbenmn: k w/e

grtbenmn: r we bff again?

thelid1: J

grtbenmn: dont ignore me agin, k?

thelid1: sry bout that . . . I guess I was just jealous u were talking to sarah

thelid1: but forget bout that . . .

grtbenmn: u were? y?

thelid1: i need ur help

grtbenmn: wussup?

thelid1: idk . . . i was being dumb

thelid1: anyhoo . . . long story

thelid1: the situation is that im being blamed for stealing and vandalizing . . .

grtbenmn: what!!!???

thelid1: and i need ur help to clear my name

grtbenmn: what can i do?

thelid1: idk

thelid1: i was hoping u would have an idea . . . let me tell u more

Lydia explained the entire situation to him—even her true feelings about the Olivers—starting with the bombing and ending with the paint can.

grtbenmn: shouldn't u b trying to figure out who bombed the guesthouse instead of who stole the money?

thelid1: don't u watch the news?

thelid1: some radical muslim group claimed responsibility for that

thelid1: my dad says they were probably not targeting the olivers

thelid1: there are lots of jewish people around there

grtbenmn: oh

grtbenmn: well, u really need to interview ppl who live near CHC

thelid1: i cant go over there anymore

grtbenmn: sarah can

thelid1: oh . . . shes back

thelid1: she says hi

grtbenmn: hi

grtbenmn: what kind of paint is it

thelid1: spray paint

grtbenmn: duh . . . what brand?

Sarah was out of breath, and Lydia reached for the spray paint can in her purse and handed it to Sarah. "You look, I'll type." She put her fingers on the keyboard. "Just don't let anyone see that paint. Get ready to drop it in your bag if anyone comes."

"Right." Sarah read off the letters—they were in English—and Lydia typed out the brand name to Ben.

thelid1: y do u need that?

grtbenmn: idk . . . ill think about it

grtbenmn: brb

thelid1: kk

Lydia felt good again. Along with Mitri, she had three friends who believed in her and were willing to help her prove her innocence. She couldn't imagine how Jesus must have felt when his best friends ran off as soon as trouble came his way.

Lydia signed off and then the girls ran outside to shove the paint can deep into the trashcan.

15
Bombed

Where are you going?" Frank asked, coming around the corner of the lobby.

Lydia tried not to cringe. "Just outside for some fresh air."

"You sure you weren't leaving? You looked like you were surprised to see me. And you know I told you to stay h—"

"Dad! I was just . . . not expecting you back yet. That's why I looked surprised."

Frank looked like maybe he didn't believe her. "Well, I need you to stay here a while longer. I'm going over to the Christian Hope Center. Mrs. Klein said you could stay here even though Sarah and her dad have to go run an errand. After that we'll get a late dinner."

Lydia nodded.

He took off his sunglasses and looked at her. "Do not leave the Shalom Guesthouse. Got it?"

Lydia nodded.

"Do you understand?"

"Yes, Dad!" she said, sounding exasperated. But she felt bad for lying to her dad.

"Okay, now give Sarah her money back."

Lydia pulled the money out of her purse, and Sarah quickly stuffed it in her pocket.

Frank left, and then a minute later Mr. Klein came to get Sarah.

Lydia groaned. She would rather be back at the Nativity Hotel with Mitri. She went and sat in the corner of the lobby, but once she got there she still didn't know what to do. The lobby was still mostly deserted, though the manager was back at the front desk. Lydia picked up her cell phone and dialed Amy's number, but she hung up when she remembered Indianapolis was seven hours behind. Amy was just about to have lunch at school.

Lydia skimmed through her small address book and saw that her dad had programmed in Cynthia's number. This older gentle-woman wasn't just Frank's boss, she was Lydia's friend. This sixty-year-old African-American woman was as smart as she was kind. As executive director GRO, she oversaw its work in dozens of countries as effortlessly as she baked chocolate chip cookies for her grandchildren. This was just the person Lydia needed to talk to.

Lydia hit the number and listened to the ring tone.

"Hello," Cynthia's voice said.

"Hi, Cynthia. This is Lydia Barnes."

"Child! Is that you?" Lydia couldn't have gotten a happier response even from Amy if she had been home. Cynthia was obviously delighted to hear from her "newfound granddaughter" and asked all kinds of questions about the trip. But she also quickly moved the conversation to a more personal level.

"What's going on?" Cynthia asked, almost as if she knew Lydia needed someone to talk to about her struggle.

"It's a horrible feeling, not being trusted," Cynthia said after Lydia had told all. "I recall a time when I was a waitress way back in high school and was accused of stealing another waitress's tip money. It was quite painful."

"How did they find out the truth?" Lydia asked. She was walking back and forth in the lobby of the guesthouse, seeing

Cynthia in her mind's eye—a tall, beautiful woman who always dressed in classy clothes.

"They didn't. To this day my old friend Carolyn must think I owe her a buck fifty." Cynthia laughed.

But Lydia couldn't stand it. She slammed herself into a chair and pulled her legs up to hug. "How do you live with that? Having people think bad about you when you didn't do anything wrong?"

"I guess by realizing that though I may be right on that issue, I *am* guilty of other things. We've all sinned, child."

"Oh." Lydia didn't have anything to say to that. She thought of how she had been keeping secrets from her dad, like betting with Sarah and finding the paint can.

Cynthia rattled on about other youthful blunders she'd made. They must have talked for an hour, and by the end of it Lydia felt much better.

A few minutes after Lydia hung up, her cell phone rang. A picture of Frank appeared on the screen and the caller ID said "World's Greatest Dad." She flipped it open.

"Hi."

Then she heard a bunch of loud voices on the other end followed by a click. She quickly set the phone down. Then . . .

BOOM!

✝ ✝ ✝

Lydia ran to the window and looked outside. A bus was on fire—right there in front of the guesthouse! People were getting up off the ground and scattering from the vehicle. Smoke was coming out of the windows. Another bomb!

Lydia was about to turn away to run to the front desk to tell someone that her dad was out there somewhere! And then she saw him. Rather than moving away from the bus, Frank was moving toward its door. When he stepped onto the bus, Lydia screamed and banged on the window, but no one could hear her.

"Dad!"

A moment later Frank appeared in the shattered doorway of the bus. He was carrying a screaming toddler in one arm and supporting a young woman with the other. The woman had her arm around his shoulder and blood drenched the side of her face. He led her through the doorway and stopped a few feet from the burning vehicle.

"Dad!" Lydia yelled again. "Get away from there!"

But he just knelt down on the side of the road and helped the woman. Lydia stood there paralyzed with fear, waiting for the bus to blow up.

People were running helter-skelter all around Frank and the injured woman. The bus simmered like a wet newspaper in a campfire. Lydia finally remembered to breathe. And then to move. She ran out the front door of the guesthouse.

Sarah and her family were standing among the crowd watching. Sarah was clinging to her dad's arm and crying. Lydia ran right past them, straight to her own dad.

"Call for help," he said when he saw her.

"9-1-1?" she asked, grabbing her cell phone from her pocket.

"No, 1-0-1." He sounded perfectly calm, just as he had on the plane on their way to Liberia a month ago when she thought they were going to crash.

The person who answered the line spoke in another language, probably Hebrew, but Lydia blurted out in English anyway. "There's been a bomb!"

"Where are you, dear?" the lady asked calmly in accented English.

Lydia kept yelling. "We're in the Jewish Quarter, near the Dung Gate. Right by the Shalom Guesthouse."

As soon as she hung up, she ran over to the toddler her dad had pulled from the bus. The boy was still sobbing hysterically. "Ima!" he cried. The first syllable was not quite an *ee* and not quite an *eye* sound. He must have been calling for his mother. Lydia picked him up and tried to soothe him. Her heart was beating faster than a drum solo, and her face must have looked like it did the day her dad told her he was Santa Claus, so it's possible that the kid didn't feel too comforted. He kept crying and reaching for his mother, who was lying on the ground moaning. Frank leaned over her supporting her head with one arm, his shirt soaked in blood.

Lydia didn't quite know what to do. She decided to quit looking around for terrorists and focus on this little guy who was even more afraid than she was. She took deep breaths and stared into the toddler's eyes, and even managed to smile. He was Israeli, and extremely beautiful. His long lashes held his tears for an instant before they spilled from his eyes. Lydia began to rock him slowly from side to side right beside his mother. "Your mama's going to be just fine," she said over and over.

A moment later the ambulance screeched to a halt nearby, siren blaring. A burly paramedic pushed Frank aside to take care of the mother. Another paramedic was helping a Palestinian man who was hurt, and Lydia immediately thought of Mitri's dad, who was living in Jerusalem. She prayed this wasn't him.

As the paramedics lifted the mother into the ambulance, Lydia rushed over to them, carrying the frightened child. "Wait! This is her little boy."

"He cannot come with us," the paramedic said, sounding as if Lydia had just asked him to miraculously heal the injured people.

"What am I supposed to do with him?" Lydia looked over at her dad, who was back at the bus helping the people there put out the fire with extinguishers from one of the nearby stores.

When she turned back, the ambulance door slammed in her face and the little boy started screaming again. "Ima!"

Lydia felt a wave of anger rush over her. She was sick of people not listening to her. She ran to the driver's side of the ambulance and knocked on the window. The man waved his hand at her as he would wave away a crazy idea and turned on the siren. Lydia quickly moved in front of the ambulance.

"No!" she yelled. "You can't go."

That got their attention. A police officer came running over and demanded to know what Lydia was doing. Frank came running as well.

"This little boy needs his mother," Lydia said loudly.

"The mother is in the ambulance?" the police officer asked.

"Yes!"

"Is there any other family here?"

"We don't know," Frank said, taking over. He put his arm around Lydia. "It doesn't look like it."

"We'll take the child to the hospital, and we will find the rest of the family," the officer said. He gently pushed Lydia and her dad out of the way of the ambulance, and it immediately rushed off. Then he called another cop over. "Take the child," he said. "Take him to the hospital, and make sure he gets connected with his mother. She's in that ambulance." Then he went back to the chaos behind them.

But when the other cop reached out for the little boy, the child clung to Lydia.

"You'll be okay," Lydia said to the little boy. "This man will take you to your mother."

She didn't know if the toddler understood her, but he finally loosened his grip and allow himself to be taken into the officer's arms.

"Thanks, miss," the officer said.

Lydia nodded but said nothing. She thought she might cry if she spoke.

As the car sped off, she looked over at her dad. He was watching her face—and smiling.

16
Misguided

Early on Friday morning, Lydia finished her breakfast and quietly walked over to the computer. It was still before dawn in Liberia, so Ben wasn't online. But Lydia was glad to see he had sent her an e-mail message.

> Lid—i could be totally wrong, but i think that brand of paint is 4 car engines . . . i found a store near where u r that sells it . . . see the pdf attached . . . Not many stores sell it. Doesnt look like there is much paint 4 sale at all . . . dont ppl paint there?

Not as far as Lydia could see. The houses were certainly unpainted. But she didn't care about that. She had a lead!

Lydia wanted to jump up and hug someone. This was great information. She could go to that store and find out who bought the paint. Ben had even provided a map. Now the mystery would easily be solved—and she would be free to go on with normal life without any false accusations against her.

Just then an IM from Sarah popped up.

> **sarhstar:** r u ok?
> **thelid1:** of course
> **sarhstar:** i cant believe what happened!
> **thelid1:** ik

thelid1: hey, we've got work 2 do

sarhstar: what?

thelid1: ben found the store where the paint was bought

thelid1: its out ur way

thelid1: we have 2 go there and find out who bought it

sarhstar: wow

sarhstar: how'd he do that?

thelid1: hes ben

thelid1: J

thelid1: so, uh, will u tell me what ben and you were talking about the other day . . .

thelid1: when he was scared about something

sarhstar: oh, hes going to meet his birth mom

sarhstar: his fam is going back to the states in the spring and his American dad has asked to meet him

thelid1: he told u that?

sarhstar: yeah . . . this whole adoption thing has been eating at him lately and he just wanted to talk about it

sarhstar: he wants 2 go 2 korea 2 c his mom but his parents r saying no

thelid1: oh

thelid1: k

thelid1: tx for telling me

sarhstar: no prob

thelid1: gotta go

thelid1: ill try to get over there soon

Ben hadn't told *her* about being adopted. Lydia figured he was, of course, since he had Asian features and his parents didn't, but he could have talked about it with her. He was definitely one of her best friends, but for some reason he was blabbing his secrets to a complete stranger instead of to her.

✝ ✝ ✝

Fifteen minutes later Lydia was sitting with Mitri in the lobby of the Nativity Hotel when her dad showed up for breakfast. Lydia jumped up. "Let's go," she said. She waved to Mitri and started for her room.

"What are you talking about?" Frank said, not moving. "Where? I'm hungry."

"Didn't you say today was our day off?" Lydia stopped in the middle of the staircase that led up to their rooms, looking back at him. "Can I go to Sarah's?"

"No," he said. "I was thinking we would go down into the Negev and rent a jeep. Oh, that reminds me. I forgot my international driver's license. I'll come up with you." He bounded up the steps behind Lydia.

Lydia walked more slowly now, blocking his way. "Off-roading again, Dad?" Their last off-roading experience had been with Ben in Africa, and the guys had liked it much better than she had.

"Come on, Lydia," he said, pushing her forward. "It'll be fun. We'll get to see more of this country that way too."

"Fine," Lydia said, but refused to be budged from the top step. "But could I please, please, please go visit Sarah first? She wants to show me a cool store near her house."

Frank shook his head. "No, Lydia. That's not a good idea." He looked at her knowingly, and she thought of his "for your own protection" line from yesterday. Little did he know this *was* for her own protection.

"Dad," she said looking down at him on the steps below her, "if you think I did it just tell me."

"I'm not saying that."

They glared at each other for a moment, and then suddenly he swept her up and carried her over his shoulder like he used to do when she was a little girl. He carried her all the way down the hall to the room.

She screamed and giggled, both loving the attention and hating being treated like a kid. "Dadd-y-y-y!"

When he set her down at the door, Lydia was still giggling and he was out of breath. He put a hand on her shoulder and said, "Fine."

"Fine what?"

"You win. If I trust you, I let you go with Sarah. And I do trust you." He said the words, but Lydia could see it took great effort. Still, his actions were true to his word. An hour later he dropped her off at Sarah's. "Let's meet back here at eleven," he said. "Take your cell phone . . . and stick together."

Sarah stuck out her hand for a cab. The store Ben had told them about was a few miles away, and she had no intention of footing it.

Lydia felt only a twinge of guilt. After all, Sarah was taking her to a store, just as Lydia had told her dad. Right?

The store turned out to be just a small hardware store, not much different from what Lydia might have expected to find in the States. And she went into hardware stores all the time. Her dad loved building things—toys, robots, go-carts, remote-controlled airplanes. Frank was a regular inventor, and Lydia helped him out in the garage all the time. "I've got the only kid on the block who knows how to use a compound miter saw," her dad once raved.

The storeowner was Israeli. He came around the counter toward them. "Can I help you?"

Sarah nudged Lydia.

"Um, yes," Lydia said. "I'm wondering if you sell this kind of paint?" She held up a piece of paper with the brand name written on it.

"I do," he said slowly, "but I don't have any here right now. Would you like to order some?"

Lydia shook her head. "No, it's okay. Do you remember when you ran out?"

The man looked at Lydia suspiciously. "Why do you want to know?"

"Umm . . . it's kind of hard to explain," she said.

"Try," the man said. He put his elbows on the counter and rested his chin in one hand.

"Well, someone spray-painted someone else's house—"

"Vandalism?" The man stood up straight again and started to walk away. "Do not include me in this."

"Wait!" Lydia said. "They think I did it—"

He turned sharply to look at her. "Did you?"

"No!" Lydia said. "I want to find out who did!"

The man sighed. "So you won't get blamed?"

Lydia nodded.

"Fine," he said. "I will go see." He went to his computer and punched in some information.

Lydia held her breath.

"We have been out of that paint for weeks. When did the crime take place?"

"Yesterday. Do you happen to remember who bought the last of it?"

"I don't remember, but it should be recorded here somewhere." The man clicked at the keyboard a moment longer and then glanced at Lydia. "Here," he said, pushing a permanent marker and a piece of paper that had been sitting on the counter toward her. "I help you, you help me. Write 'Help Wanted' on this paper and hang it on the door."

Lydia wrote the letters as neatly as she could—she would have made a hundred copies and hung them all over town if he'd requested that. The paper moved onto a sticky spot on the counter and Lydia quickly licked her finger to wipe the spot off; but all she managed was to smudge the letters and get ink on her fingers.

"Good enough," the man said. He handed her a roll of tape. "Now go hang it."

That took Lydia just a second and she was back at the counter.

"It was a car dealer," the man said. "He uses that kind of paint for his engines."

"He paints engines red?"

"Red? No, I have that product only in black."

Lydia felt like a kid who had been next in line for the roller coaster when the park closed. "Well, thanks anyway." She and Sarah began to walk out of the store.

"Wait," the storeowner said. "I know of a little shop that might sell this." He scribbled out a map on a piece of scrap paper and handed it to Lydia.

Sarah peeked over her shoulder. "That's Palestinian territory, Lydia," she whispered. "I don't go there, remember?"

"You could just buy from me some regular paint and clean up the damage," the man suggested, going back to his work.

"Then they'd really think I did it!" Lydia said.

The man shrugged. "Suit yourself."

As they waited for a cab, Sarah's stubbornness returned. "I'm not going there, Lydia."

"Why not?"

"Jewish people don't go into Palestinian territory. I never have and I never will."

"Why not? Aren't you allowed?"

"We're allowed, but . . ."

"But what?"

Sarah didn't say anything.

"It just doesn't seem right," Lydia said sharply.

"What?"

"This whole . . . conflict." She didn't know how else to say it.

"It's just the way it is, Lydia."

A cab drove into sight and Sarah waved at it.

"Why do Jews and Palestinians hate each other so much?" Lydia asked. "It seems like there wouldn't be so much terrorism if you guys could just be at peace."

Sarah's eyes flashed. "Who are you to talk? You don't have peace, either. Look at you, running all over town to right this one little wrong. What if you had lived with this threat for your whole life? You don't like being . . . ehr . . . falsely accused? So why don't you just . . . ehr . . . take the blame? That would solve everything." Lydia could tell Sarah was stressed, because her English was getting worse. "It's not so easy as you think to live in this country. You just don't understand."

The cab pulled over and Sarah climbed in. Lydia followed.

Lydia gave the address of the Palestinian store she wanted to go to. Sarah's eyes narrowed as she whipped her head around to glare at Lydia. "I said I'm not going there!" she hissed. She turned to the driver and gave the guesthouse address.

17
Convicted

The second they arrived at the Shalom Guesthouse, Lydia tore out of the cab. She didn't want to be anyplace near Sarah. She went to sit on the patio and Sarah went indoors.

"Ms. Barnes?"

Lydia turned around to face whoever had called her. Lydia didn't recognize the woman at first—a tall American dressed in olive green cargo pants and a black cotton jacket. But then Lydia saw the hand-decorated glasses and realized it was the Bible teacher who was leading Marcus's group. Lydia quickly looked around for Marcus, but Dr. Erwin was clearly alone.

"Sorry," Dr. Erwin said, "it's just me. But perhaps this will make up for that." She pulled something out of her pocket. "Marcus asked me to deliver this to you on my way out of town. I needed to talk to your dad anyway. I didn't realize you were no longer staying here, so I'm glad I caught you."

Lydia's eyes grew wide. Dr. Erwin was handing her a beautiful silver bracelet with a bejeweled spike pendant. From Marcus! It looked familiar somehow. He must have bought it at a shop here in Jerusalem. In other words . . . he bought it just for her!

"Thank you," Lydia said, looking at the bracelet in her hands. "Thank you so much. Did he say anything?"

"No. Just, 'Can you give this to Lydia?'" Dr. Erwin said. "He gets points for effort, at least." She grinned.

Lydia grinned back. "I'll say."

"So, is your dad here?" Dr. Erwin asked.

"No—but, hey!" Lydia had a brainstorm. "He gave me permission to go to a store with my friend, but she can't go anymore." *Wouldn't* go was more like it. "I can't go alone. Would you be willing to go with me? Maybe my dad will be here by the time we get back."

Dr. Erwin looked at her watch. "Well, I have a few minutes. Where is it?"

Lydia handed her the map, and the woman nodded. "Sure. That's not too far. Let's grab a cab."

"So, what store are we heading for?" Dr. Erwin asked once they had gotten into a cab and were on their way.

"It's a hardware store," Lydia said. "I need to check on something."

Dr. Erwin didn't say anything, and Lydia was glad she wasn't asking questions. At one point, Dr. Erwin turned to look at the valley below them. "That's the Pool of Siloam down there."

Lydia leaned over to look. The slopes leading down into the valley were packed with the typical rectangular white homes and apartments of this city, but she could see a large patch of green at the bottom. Lydia didn't know what the Pool of Siloam was, but she expected Dr. Erwin would tell her.

"Jesus once placed mud on a blind man's eyes and told him to go wash in the Pool of Siloam."

"Oh yeah!" Lydia said. "And then he could see."

Dr. Erwin nodded. "Right. When we listen to Jesus—when we really hear him—we can see. It's quite amazing."

Lydia nodded, feeling a bit confused.

"You're doing something important, aren't you?" Dr. Erwin said.

Lydia nodded. It was *so* important that she was willing to beg a virtual stranger to travel through this bomb-infested city with her. "I've got to clear my name."

Dr. Erwin waited.

"My dad thinks I was involved in the mess at the Christian Hope Center. Did you hear about that?"

"Not about you being involved, but I did hear about it. Why does he think you're involved? You don't seem to be the type."

"I'm not." Lydia described what was going on and why she was going to this other hardware store.

"This *is* important," Dr. Erwin said seriously.

Lydia grinned, understanding why this lady got along so well with her dad. She took kids seriously.

"Sure," the owner said. He lifted lightbulbs from his cart and placed them on the shelves while he talked. "I remember who bought that paint. We not sell so much red paint, and not just one can."

This hardware store was a bit bigger than the one Lydia had gone to with Sarah, but it was all the same stuff. The other one was not as neat as this one either. Here, everything was organized and labeled.

"Who was it?" Lydia asked eagerly.

"A young person," he said without even looking at her. He was reaching up high to put a stack of small bulbs in place. Dr. Erwin, who was taller, reached up and did it for him.

"What did he look like?" Lydia asked.

"Boy, girl—I do not know," the storeowner said. "It was a kid in jeans, sweatshirt, and a blue ball cap."

"Did the person pay with check or credit card? Could you look up the name?"

The shopkeeper chuckled. "People here not use checks or credit cards. Only cash. This kid pay in American dollars."

As she and Dr. Erwin walked out of the store, Lydia sighed. "I guess I've got to let this go. I'm just not a good enough detective." She wished Ben were here. He'd know what to do.

"Unfortunately every clue you're coming up with is just pointing the finger at you," Dr. Erwin said.

Lydia hesitated at the door of the cab that had been waiting. "What do you mean?"

"A paint can in your trash. A kid your age who bought the paint."

Lydia stared at her. "Now *you* think I did it?"

Dr. Erwin smiled. "Not at all." She opened the door of the cab for Lydia and held out a hand to usher her in. "I'm saying that your reputation is in God's hands. By trying to prove your innocence, you may be setting yourself up. This is going to come down to your character, not absolute proof."

Lydia ducked into the car, and Dr. Erwin closed the door behind Lydia.

"Aren't you coming?" Lydia asked through the open window.

"I'll catch another," Dr. Erwin said. "I'm heading another direction. And I've really got to get going."

"Okay. Well, thanks for the help," Lydia said. "Will you come to see me and my dad later? We're staying at the Nativity Hotel in Bethlehem now."

"Actually, I'm going home now—"

"You are?" Lydia had thought Marcus would be staying through Christmas. She wanted to see him again.

"Don't worry. Everyone else is staying. Including Marcus." She winked.

"So why are you leaving?"

Dr. Erwin sighed. "I have a family emergency."

"Oh. I'm sorry. What's wrong?"

"Nothing you have to worry about," she said kindly. "But thanks. This cab will take you straight back to the guesthouse. Are you comfortable with that?"

Lydia smiled. "Yeah, I'm okay. Thanks for your help."

The cab pulled away. Lydia sat in the backseat, knowing she was never going to find the culprit. Maybe that was for the best. She thought of what Dr. Erwin had said as they'd passed by the Pool of Siloam: When we listen to Jesus, we can see.

"That's it," she whispered. "I need to hear what Jesus says to me. I need to do what He says." She sat up straight and smiled. "I'm going to forgive my enemies. No more trying to nail this kid who set me up." After all, her dad would love her even if he thought she was guilty, but anyone who really could do such bad things desperately needed forgiveness. And if it was Brenda or even Marcus, how could she get them in trouble anyway?

She looked at her watch. Her dad had said to be back by 11:00, and it wasn't even 10:30 yet. She smiled. It felt good to be good.

18
Framed

She ditched me," Sarah said, sitting comfortably in a cushy chair in the guesthouse lobby. Lydia's dad stood beside Sarah's chair.

Lydia wanted to scream. She wanted to blurt out that, yeah, well, Sarah made a bet when she wasn't supposed to! She didn't, though. She kept quiet. So her face probably looked like an egg in a microwave just before it pops.

"Is that true, Lydia?" Frank asked Lydia. "Did you really ditch Sarah and then go out into the city on your own?"

"No. We went to the store, just like we said. We came back here, and then I went with Dr. Erwin to another store."

"Dr. Erwin?" her dad asked.

"Yes. You can even ask her."

Frank nearly growled as he pulled his phone out of his front shirt pocket. "I *will* ask her."

Frank used the wireless Internet feature on his phone to look up a number, then dialed. Lydia could hear the ringing, and then the voice of the operator at Novotel saying that Dr. Erwin had checked out that morning. "Ah, we're sad to tell you that Dr. Erwin had to return home early this morning for a family emergency."

Lydia nodded as Frank hung up. "Yes! She said she was going back for a family emergency. She's on her way to the airport now!"

"The game's up, Lydia," Frank said in a voice that showed this was anything but fun and games. "And now we have a serious problem on our hands."

"But, Dad! I'm telling you exactly what the hotel told you. Why don't you believe me?"

"Yes, you told me what you *heard* the hotel tell me. And you couldn't have gone to some store with Dr. Erwin, because she left this morning."

"Just because she checked out this morning doesn't mean she went right to the airpor—"

"That's *enough*, Lydia." He said it in that way that meant she'd better do it or else.

Lydia looked at the floor. She didn't want to look at Sarah, and she didn't know what to say.

"Sit out there," he said, pointing to the patio chairs where Lydia had been sitting when Dr. Erwin had showed up. "I have to make a couple calls, and then we're going to have a long talk."

Lydia turned around and walked out the front door of the guesthouse. She sat in one of the lawn chairs just as she was told and tried to keep her heart from jumping out of her chest. The sun was out and it didn't feel as cold as the fifty-seven degrees the TV weatherman had said it would be, but Lydia still pulled her arms tightly around herself.

As she sat there fuming she tried to think of reasons to put Sarah back on the suspect list. But even as she did it, she realized Sarah couldn't possibly be the culprit. It had to be someone who could—or would—go into Palestinian territory to buy the paint. Dr. Erwin was right. The more Lydia tried to prove herself innocent, the more guilty she looked.

She just hoped Sarah wasn't mad enough to use all their detective work to "prove" that Lydia was guilty.

The paint!

Lydia looked around. Her dad was nowhere in sight and Sarah had left the lobby. She jumped up and ran to the trashcan. More junk had been piled on top, so it was totally gross—but Lydia was desperate. She pushed her sleeve up and reached in—and touched something slimy. When she pulled her hand out, her arm brushed up against more slime, and she almost screamed. A second later a whiff of something like rotten eggs mixed with baby poop blasted her nose, and she almost puked.

She held her breath and tried to imagine that all the goop she was sticking her fingers into was pudding or soap or bubble bath—until her fingers landed on something hard and metal. She pulled out the paint can and almost kissed it. She wasn't that dumb, though. She wiped it—and her fingers—on a napkin and then put it under her sweater.

A minute later her dad came out and found Lydia sitting with her hands folded on the table, as sweet as an angel.

They hailed a cab and got in. Frank directed the driver to take them to the Nativity Hotel in Bethlehem. Then he leaned back and sighed as if someone had just died.

"What?" she asked. She wanted to sound mean, but her voice came out whiny instead. She really did hate hurting her dad's feelings. She just wished he would believe her. Of *course* she would never do anything as terrible as stealing and vandalizing.

"The Lighthouse was vandalized yesterday," her dad said.

"The Lighthouse?" Lydia couldn't believe it. As awful as she knew the crimes against the Christian Hope Center were, she sort of understood why people didn't like the Olivers. But Jordan and Claire and the gang, they were cool! "What happened?"

"A bunch of the photos were scribbled on with marker."

"Claire's photos?"

"Yeah," Frank said. He glanced over at her. "Show me your hands."

Lydia jumped. "What?"

"Show me."

She held out her hands, and saw, the same time her father did, the ink on her fingers from the hardware store. "Ink," he said.

And then the paint can shifted under her sweater.

"What's that?"

She hugged herself to stop him from looking, but he reached over and touched it. "Show me."

Lydia almost cried as she pulled the can out and handed it to him.

Her dad looked as though he had just seen an olive tree morph into a giant spider—and Lydia couldn't tell if he was more horrified or terrified. "It's not what it looks like, Dad!" she said grabbing him by the arm, desperate to make him believe her.

Still, he said nothing. He simply stared at the can in his hands. Finally he looked at her. "Give me the markers now."

"Dad! I didn't do it!" She held out her hands and tried to show him that she had nothing else to hide.

He dropped the paint can into his bag. "What's that on your wrist?"

Oh no. Lydia hadn't told him she got a present from a boy. This was the worst timing ever. "It was a gift," she said, holding her wrist close to her body.

Frank didn't look away from her. "From who?"

Lydia thought quickly. "Dr. Erwin gave it to me."

"Dr. Erwin?"

"Yes." Lydia looked out the window at the crowd of people they were passing and wished she could disappear into it.

"Lydia, let me see that bracelet."

Lydia sighed loudly to show how annoyed she was, but she held it up. He pulled it up close to his face, as if he were looking for something. Lydia looked too—and realized why it looked so familiar. The bracelet perfectly matched the bracelets at the Olivers' bookstore. There was one difference, though. The bracelets in the display case had a cross on them, but hers had only a spike. Lydia remembered the broken piece Mr. Oliver had found on the floor, and she knew that the mystery of the broken cross was solved.

Her dad must have realized it too. He set her arm down and remained quiet for a moment. "I didn't want to believe it," he finally said.

The cab worked its way through the busy traffic, and Lydia could see they were getting closer to the checkpoint. She could feel her chest tighten as the panic inside her grew. She wanted to blame it all on Sarah, but there was no way Sarah could have gone to Bethlehem, deep in Palestinian territory. And it wasn't Sarah who had given her the bracelet.

But the culprit couldn't be Marcus!

"Where did you and Mitri go yesterday?" her dad asked quietly without looking at her.

"We went to the Jacir Palace Hotel. We weren't anywhere near the Lighthouse."

"And where did you go just now after you ditched Sarah?"

"I went to a store to find out who bought this paint!" Lydia said desperately. "Dr. Erwin was there. You have to believe me! You said you would believe me!"

Her dad was quiet while they went through the checkpoint. When the cab pulled over in front of the Nativity Hotel, they got out and he paid the driver. The cab drove away and Frank finally turned to Lydia. "I can't protect you anymore. You have to be accountable for your actions."

Any other dad would get her out of the country ASAP if he thought his daughter was about to go to jail. Lydia's dad picked up the phone to set up a meeting with the people who were throwing her in.

"I hoped it wasn't true," he said quietly into the phone, "but I have found more evidence against her."

After a few minutes of mainly listening, Frank hung up the phone and turned to Lydia. "Tomorrow you need to confess and apologize so that we can move forward. Any more lying and you'll just be digging yourself deeper."

"But I didn't do it." She wasn't about to lie and say she'd done something when she hadn't. She wasn't going to take the blame for someone else's crime. Maybe Jesus could do that kind of thing. He at least knew He was going to rise again from the dead—but who knew what would happen to her?

"I'm serious, Lydia. They told me they will press charges— unless you are willing to apologize, return the money, and scrub off the paint. Oh, and pay for the bracelet."

They were at the checkpoint now, and their conversation was put on hold as the guards checked the glove box and looked at passports. Lydia could see the driver was agitated, just as all the drivers were, but she was just tired of the whole thing. As soon as they started moving again, Lydia mumbled, "I just want to go home and have a normal Christmas with stockings and Christmas lights. I want to see Amy. I want to see Grandma. I don't want to be here." It was hard to talk while she was crying, and her words jerked out of her. "What a lousy Christmas."

"Yes, young lady," Frank growled, "it certainly is."

19
Desperate

Take the deal."

It was an hour later, and Lydia was back at the Nativity Hotel. She and Mitri were in the lobby, sitting on the floor against the wall.

"Take the deal." Mitri said again when Lydia shrugged. "All they want is for you to apologize, return the money, and scrub off the paint? Why wouldn't you take the deal?"

"Because I didn't do it!" Didn't anyone believe her?

"What difference does it make?" Mitri said. "They think it's your fault and they'll arrest you if you don't take responsibility. Trust me, you don't want that."

Lydia sighed. "I don't even have the money to give back."

"I have some money," Mitri said. "How much do you need?"

Lydia was touched. "Too much—250 shekels. But I'm not taking your money." She smiled at him. "I do think it was very sweet of you to offer." Then she sighed and picked up her cell phone. "I need to call Sarah."

"I thought—"

"I know. But I don't want to fight anymore. And I really was stupid for trying to get her to go with me to those stores."

Lydia leaned forward and sat cross-legged on the hard floor. Mitri rested his head back against the wall.

Sarah answered on the third ring.

Saying sorry wasn't as hard as Lydia thought it would be. She really did regret pressuring Sarah to go to Bethlehem, so apologizing for it came easily.

"It's okay," Sarah said right away. "I don't blame you. So what did you find out?"

Lydia told her everything about Dr. Erwin and the hardware store and how her dad didn't believe her.

"That's awful, Lydia," Sarah said very slowly when Lydia had finished. "But you need to take the deal."

"I know," Lydia said miserably. "I'm going to ask my dad if I can borrow the money from him and earn it back somehow."

"I have money," Sarah said.

Lydia couldn't believe how generous her friends were. She heard rustling coming from Sarah's side of the phone conversation. "What are you doing?"

"I'm putting 250 shekels in an envelope. I'll leave it at the front desk for you in case I'm not here when you come by."

"No, Sarah," Lydia said. "I'm not taking your money."

The rustling stopped. There was silence for a moment. Then Sarah said, "Lydia, I'm sorry for telling on you to your dad."

"It's okay," Lydia said with a grin, glad she wasn't the only one messing up. "Everybody makes mistakes."

"Okay, come on," Lydia said to Mitri as soon as she was off the phone. She ran to the computer and logged on, hoping desperately that Ben would be online. She just had to know for sure if it was Marcus who had done the spray painting, and she had an idea.

Ben was on.

grtbenmn: hey lid
thelid1: ben!
thelid1: i need u!
grtbenmn: course u do
grtbenmn: J
thelid1: will you search for pics of marcus online
thelid1: to see if u can find one of him with a blue ball hat
thelid1: the kid who bought the paint wore one
thelid1: can u look?
grtbenmn: course i can look
thelid1: oh my gosh i luv u
grtbenmn: course u do
grtbenmn: J
thelid1: how long will it take?
grtbenmn: uh . . . forever
grtbenmn: you said can i not will i
grtbenmn: J

Lydia turned her head to stare at Mitri in disbelief. "I'm on death row here and he's checking my grammar?"

Mitri smiled. "Some of us enjoy using the English language properly."

Lydia smiled.

"Besides, we might have fun scrubbing the Christian center."

grtbenmn: sry
grtbenmn: im not a miracle worker

Lydia hardly read Ben's words. She looked back at Mitri. "We? Wait. What are you talking about?"

"Dad just told me he got approval for me to go to Jerusalem. He had been planning for me to go out there for Christmas before you even mentioned it." His dark eyes were bright. "I'll ask him if I can use the permission to cross over for this."

"You can't do that!" Lydia said. "If you go over there you, have to go see your dad's place and explore the city and all that!" Lydia got a lump in her throat. She had been feeling like the world was against her, but now three friends were standing beside her.

"Well, maybe I can do that too," he said.

"Lydia," Frank said, walking in the door. "I need to talk to you." He didn't sound happy.

Lydia logged out without an explanation to Ben and followed her dad upstairs. He hadn't talked to her the entire ride back to Bethlehem, and she was desperate to hear what he had to say, no matter what.

✝ ✝ ✝

"I talked to Dr. Erwin." Lydia's dad was standing by the door of the hotel room and Lydia was sitting on the edge of the bed.

Lydia jumped up. "You did! Well, that's wonderful! That means—"

"That means I owe you an apology," Frank said. "You have been honest with me this whole time, and I didn't trust you."

Lydia looked down. She hadn't been totally honest. She had lied about the bet money and she had snuck off to the Novotel and she had gone off to hardware stores without telling him.

"I know you made mistakes too, Peachoo," he said, as if reading her mind. "But I know you didn't steal that money or vandalize anything. I'm asking you to forgive me for doubting you."

Lydia ran over to hug him. "I forgive you! And I don't blame you at all. I sure looked guilty. Oh, but, Dad! I'm so glad. I couldn't bear it anymore."

After a long hug, Frank pulled away. "Now, we still need to work out a couple things. First, you are not old enough to date. Especially not a boy like him."

"A boy like him? What do you mean?"

"Lydia, don't you see? He must have done all the things you're being accused of."

"No, he wouldn't do that, Dad. He's not like that."

"All the evidence shows—"

"Dad, all the evidence showed I was guilty too."

"Well, we'll see. But you're still not old enough to date."

Lydia sulked, but not for long. Frank was on to other business.

"We also need to keep our appointment with the Olivers."

"What?"

"We need to clear the air with them. And with Jordan."

"Jordan?"

"From the Lighthouse. He thinks you did the graffiti at his place too." Lydia groaned, but Frank went on. "How did you get marker on your hand, by the way?"

"I made a help-wanted sign at the hardware store for the owner guy."

"Oh. Well. I will request that we meet at the Lighthouse rather than the Christian Hope Center. I think you'll feel more comfortable there."

Comfortable. Yeah, right. Lydia pictured going into a tiny room, blindfolded, with a bare lightbulb swinging from a cord over her head, and answering tormenting questions. She could hardly wait.

Lydia couldn't quit wiggling nervously, even when her dad glared at her and Mitri jabbed her in the ribs with his elbow.

It was Sunday morning, Christmas Eve, and they were worshipping at the Church of Saint Catherine in Bethlehem. When they'd walked over to the church that morning, Lydia had stared at the huge sign painted on the wall under the Israeli guard tower. The sign proclaimed peace on earth—with armed guards watching from above. Sure, she was sitting in church singing carols, but this was not a normal Christmas.

Besides, they were meeting with the Olivers and Jordan afterward, and Lydia knew her dad's plan wouldn't work. How could they clear the air? Mrs. Oliver would not smile sweetly and say, "Oh, okay then." She was more likely to dance on the hump of a galloping camel than believe Lydia was innocent.

And so Lydia wiggled.

"What do you have to say for yourself, young lady?" Mrs. Oliver demanded the moment they were all seated.

Lydia wasn't under a lightbulb, but she was still sweating. Everyone was there: Mr. and Mrs. Oliver, Brenda, Jordan, Claire. And they were all staring at her with anger in their eyes. Lydia knew they'd never believe her, and she felt sad to lose the friendship of both Brenda and Claire.

They were at the Lighthouse in a meeting room Lydia hadn't seen before. There were about four couches and various chairs spread in sort of a circle. She could just imagine how much fun it would be to hang out here with a bunch of the Lighthouse volunteers . . . under very different circumstances.

"Mrs. Oliver," Lydia said, "what I have to say is that I am honestly very, very, very sad about everything that's happened."

Mrs. Oliver lifted her nose and sniffed.

Lydia looked at Jordan and Claire. "And I mean that for you guys too. Claire, those pictures you took were amazing, and I can only imagine how horrified you both must be."

"You sound like a politician, Lydia," Mrs. Oliver said, cutting off the rest of Lydia's carefully planned speech. "If that's an apology then I'm a monkey's uncle."

Lydia somehow stopped herself from saying, "Well, then, my work here is done."

"I must agree," Jordan said. "We at the Lighthouse are taking this very seriously, and I wish to hear it straight."

Claire wouldn't even look up at her. Brenda did, though. She was glaring almost as angrily as Mrs. Oliver.

Lydia looked at her dad. She needed help.

The door to the room opened. Mr. Klein—Sarah's dad—walked in chatting with one of the Lighthouse volunteers. Everyone turned to look at them, and Frank called out a surprised hello. When Mr. Klein looked up, he pulled an expression that Lydia had seen on her church friends' faces when she'd run into them at the zoo or something—glad to see people you know but also confused because they are not where they belong.

And then she saw Sarah.

Sarah's expression was nothing like her dad's. She was horrified.

Lydia jumped up. "Sarah! What are you doing here? This is—" She was about to say "Palestinian territory," but she didn't want to offend Mitri. Not that it should, but she just didn't know. "Is everything okay?"

"You know each other?" Jordan asked. He stood up and went over to shake Mr. Klein's hand. "These are some of our favorite people. Jewish people who care. They see what their country is doing to its neighbors, and they offer a hand."

Mr. Klein looked embarrassed.

"He—and Sarah, of course," Jordan said with a wink to the girl who looked as embarrassed as her dad, "—come here to serve every week. They are my heroes."

Mr. Klein didn't crack a smile at this compliment. He mumbled something like, "Yes, well, back to business." And Sarah followed her dad toward the door on the other side of the room without saying a word.

Lydia's mind raced. And then everything came together.

It was Sarah.

Sarah must have followed them when Frank and Lydia had gone to the Christian Hope Center the morning the money had been stolen.

Sarah wouldn't go to the second hardware store not because it was in Palestinian territory but because she thought the owner would remember her. Because obviously she *did* go into Palestinian territory if she came here.

Yesterday on the phone when Sarah had so generously offered money, she had known exactly how much money was needed: 250 shekels. How could Sarah have known the amount if she hadn't stolen it in the first place?

As for the charm bracelet—the cross with the arms broken off—that Marcus had given Lydia—it must have been passed on from Sarah. Lydia remembered the IM chat with Marcus when he mentioned he had seen Sarah and then asked Lydia where she would be the next day. Sarah must have told him this was Lydia's bracelet and asked him to give it to her.

Which meant Marcus hadn't given the bracelet to Lydia as a

gift. It also meant Marcus was innocent. And it also meant Sarah had set Lydia up on purpose.

The girls locked eyes as all this information passed through Lydia's brain.

It all happened in an instant. And Lydia knew, in that instant, exactly what she would do.

20
At Peace

O kay," Lydia said, still locked onto Sarah's eyes. "I did it. I did it all."

Frank hollered, "What!" He was most definitely not expecting this confession.

Mitri's smile got big, and his fist squeezed tight.

Jordan let out a short laugh that sounded anything but happy. "You are making a confession?"

Mr. Oliver showed more expression than Lydia had ever seen on his face before: He raised his eyebrows.

Brenda and Claire looked at each other and exchanged a what-an-awful-child shrug.

And Sarah? Her face went from total panic to sheer relief.

✝   ✝   ✝

Mrs. Oliver broke into loud sobbing. "Why? Why?"

Lydia took a deep breath and tried to think of how to continue. "I took the money when I was alone in the bookstore. I . . . uh . . . didn't plan to. I . . . uh . . . " she hesitated, and then remembered her role as Juliet in the school play last year, and she got bolder. Everyone in the room was giving her all their attention, including her dad, who looked as confused as a city boy in a barnyard. "I . . . uh . . . stepped on the bracelet by accident. When I saw it was broken, I thought I should pay for it. But I didn't want to tell anyone, so I . . . uh . . . went to put the money in the cash register. Uh . . . when I saw all that money, I couldn't resist. I took it."

"I knew it!" Mrs. Oliver said. "And the vandalism?"

That one was harder. "I did that when I . . . uh . . . just before my dad found me by the guesthouse," she said, almost forgetting to sound sorry.

Sarah was looking down now. Lydia couldn't see her face, but she guessed she was thanking her lucky stars—and that made Lydia feel surprisingly good. Sarah might have been the culprit for these crimes, but Lydia was far from perfect herself. Jesus had taken the blame for her sins, and now Lydia realized she was glad to be able to do the same for someone else.

"So, explain where you got the paint," her dad said, standing up with his arms crossed in front of his chest. He looked at her with his eyebrows raised, as if to say, "I'll believe you when there is peace in the Middle East." She had convinced him a little too well that she was innocent.

"Oh, that," Lydia said. "I found the paint in a trashcan. And I just decided that—"

"No, Lydia! Don't do it!" It was Sarah. She ran to the front of the room and clutched Lydia's arm. "Don't say anything else." Then she turned to face everyone in the room—all of them gaping at the two girls, wondering what in the world was going on. "Lydia had nothing to do with any of the things you are accusing her of." Sarah began to cry. "I did them."

"What!" Frank said again.

Mitri cheered. Jordan's face displayed total disbelief. Mr. Oliver lowered his eyebrows. Mrs. Oliver jumped up. Claire covered her mouth with her hand. Brenda smiled at Lydia with surprise and admiration.

And Mr. Klein, Sarah's usually grumpy and distant father, ran the length of the room toward his daughter. "Sarah, no!"

He took Sarah in his arms, and Sarah wept all the more. "I'm sorry, Father. I know I shouldn't have done it. I know it was a big mistake, and I'll do anything you want to make it right again. I was mad at the Christians and mad that you were helping them. They are destroying us. They are destroying the Jewish people. And I was especially mad that you were helping the Palestinians. They are trying to kill us!"

"What have you done, Sarah?" Mr. Klein said with emotion in his voice as he stroked her hair.

Sarah looked at Mrs. Oliver. "I stole your money. I still have it, and I'll give it all back to you." She looked away. "I don't have the bracelet I took, though," she glanced at Lydia, "so I'll use my own money to buy it."

"The bracelet you broke and then stole," Mrs. Oliver corrected.

Sarah nodded morosely and then looked at Jordan.

"And I drew on those pictures," she said. She turned to Claire. "I didn't mean to hurt your feelings, but they made me so angry."

"Why?" Claire asked quietly.

"Those pictures made the Palestinian people seem so . . . real. So human. They made me feel rotten inside." She turned back to her dad, who was standing with his hand over his heart, staring at Sarah. "I'm sorry, Father," she said again. "You're so good and I'm so . . . rotten. I'll work or something to pay for what I've done."

No one seemed to know what to do next.

It was Mitri who broke the spell. He stood up and walked over to Sarah, put his hand on her shoulder until she turned to look at him, and then, smiling, reached in to give her a hug.

Jordan stood up and slowly walked toward Sarah. He hugged her too.

And then Frank.

And then Mr. Oliver.

And then Brenda and Claire.

And then even Mrs. Oliver, after sighing loudly enough to be heard over the sound of Christmas carols outside the building.

Lydia was the last one to hug Sarah, not because she was mad but because she was waiting for Sarah to look at her. When Sarah finally turned her head, Lydia was smiling. And not just a little bit. She was smiling so big she thought her face might explode.

"What are you grinning about?" Sarah asked, laughing through her tears. "Are you glad you're finally . . . ehr . . . off the hook?"

Lydia grabbed her friend in the biggest bear hug she could manage. "No. I'm glad you are."

Claire was the first one to speak to Lydia when the hug-fest was over. Mr. Klein took Sarah over to talk with Jordan and Mr. and Mrs. Oliver—probably trying to figure out what her punishment should be. Lydia was glad to be out of that circle. Frank was talking to Brenda, and Lydia was just sitting on one of the couches hugging her knees. She felt perfectly content.

"You did a very brave thing," Claire said. "You taught me a great lesson."

Lydia grinned. It felt so good to be on good terms with Claire again. "I just hope you can get new copies of your pictures."

"Oh, I can," Claire said. "That was never the problem. The real problem was my anger. But now even that is gone. If you can forgive, then I also can."

Lydia nodded. "Yeah, that's how I managed it too. I figured that if Jesus can forgive the people who killed Him, then I can forgive my friend who framed me."

"Framed you? Oh, that reminds me. I must have your photograph."

Brenda wandered over while Lydia sat there cheesing for the camera. "Can I get a copy?" Brenda asked. "I want a picture of this hero on my wall." As soon as the pose was done, Brenda leaned over and squeezed Lydia long and hard. "I'm sooo sorry for suspecting you, girl," she whispered. "I hope you'll forgive me."

"I already have," Lydia whispered back.

"My turn," Frank said. Brenda stepped back, laughing, and Frank pulled his daughter off the couch. He grabbed her in a giant bear hug, lifting her feet off the floor, and said, "I couldn't be more proud of you, Peachoo. You did a wonderful thing."

"My question," Brenda said when Frank finally put Lydia down, "is whether you guys will be sticking around. Is Global Relief and Outreach going to set up a mission here?"

"Not a chance," Frank said. "With the Christian Hope Center and the Lighthouse working together, what do you need us for? I'm taking my daughter home the day after Christmas as planned."

$$ \dagger \quad \dagger \quad \dagger $$

"I heard that they discovered hidden tunnels below the city," Mitri said as he scrubbed the guesthouse wall, "from the time of King Herod."

"Yes!" Sarah said. "I've never been to see them. We've got to go check them out!"

"You missed a spot," Lydia said to Mitri. She grinned at him.

He rolled up his towel and swatted her, laughing. "Don't ruin my perfect day in the Holy City."

It was the first time in Mitri's life that he had been out of Bethlehem, and he was spending it scrubbing paint within sight of the ancient walls of the Old City.

Sarah cringed a little. "I'm sorry you have to work instead of exploring Jerusalem."

"Would you please stop apologizing? We will get there soon enough. And I am having a good time right here!"

"Yeah," Sarah said, "it's a blast."

"Don't say that word," Lydia said. She shivered. She'd had enough blasts in this place.

Mr. Oliver walked outside and stood back to admire the work. All the red paint had come off, and they were now moving to the next wall. "That's good enough for me," Mr. Oliver said. "You kids better get yourselves off to the Old City before Christmas Day is over."

He walked over to Sarah and held out a little box. "But first, a little something for you. Don't tell the missus." He winked.

Sarah smiled and tore the box open. Inside was a bracelet like the one she had taken from them. Only the cross was not broken.

"No need to work for this," he said. "It's a gift."

Lydia watched Sarah's face carefully. Sarah certainly didn't like the cross any better than before, and Lydia wondered if she would be offended by the gift. But Sarah's smile was for real. "Thank you so much, Mr. Oliver."

"Now get out of here before I change my mind," he said, laughing.

The kids didn't need to be told twice. Lydia the American, Sarah the Israeli, and Mitri the Palestinian ran through the streets of old Jerusalem together, exploring ancient ruins and newfound friendship.

Every time Lydia stopped to think about it, she was amazed: She was in a faraway country, celebrating Christmas without snow or presents or hot chocolate beneath a decorated evergreen—but she had never felt more at home in her life. This year, Christmas was exactly as it should be.

Only one thing was missing. But soon even that niggling detail was resolved.

The three were standing in a tourist shop looking around, and Lydia was admiring a blue jewel—one that the shopkeeper said could be found only in the Middle East. "I've never seen anything so gorgeous!"

"Why, thank you," a male voice said from beside her. It was Marcus. "You're kind of cute yourself."

Lydia felt her face turn the color of Santa's coat. Mitri and Sarah didn't help any: They started laughing at her.

The teens from Marcus's tour group were teasing him too. Lydia almost died of embarrassment. "Should we leave you two alone?" one of them asked, laughing.

"Actually," Marcus said, "if you don't mind, that would be great."

Lydia almost died again.

Mitri and Sarah laughed and left the store.

Marcus seemed suddenly nervous. "Uh," he said. "Umm . . ."

Lydia waited, feeling like fireworks were going off in her brain.

"Uh . . ." he said again. "I'm just wondering if . . . well, like . . . I know we live far away from each other and everything . . ."

"Yes?" Lydia said.

"So, like, maybe you won't want to, but . . ."

Lydia laughed. "No, Marcus," she said, putting an end to his agony. "I can't go out with you. My dad would kill me! But let's definitely keep in touch."

She gave him a great big hug and he turned bright red. Suddenly Lydia saw a teenage girl she recognized. It was Michelle, Marcus's sister. She jumped up from around the corner and snapped a picture.

"Merry Christmas!" Michelle shouted.

It was. It was a very merry Christmas.